Second Watch

Second Watch

KAREN AUTIO

sononis
PRESS
WINLAW BRITISH COLUMBIA

LIBRARY AND ARCHIVES CANADA CATALOGUING IN PUBLICATION

Autio, Karen, 1958-
    Second watch / Karen Autio.

ISBN 1-55039-151-8

    1. Empress   of   Ireland   (Steamship)—Juvenile   fiction.
2. Shipwrecks—Québec (Province)—Saint   Lawrence   River
Estuary—Juvenile fiction. 3. Finns—Ontario—Thunder Bay
History—Juvenile fiction. I. Title.
PS8601.U85S42 2005   jC813'.6   C2005-901420-2

Sono Nis Press most gratefully acknowledges the support for our publishing
program provided by the Government of Canada through the Book Publishing
Industry Development Program (BPIDP), the Canada Council for the Arts, and
the British Columbia Arts Council.

Edited by Laura Peetoom
Cover painting and artwork by Briana Bach Hertzog
Chorus of "Crossing the Water" used as the epigraph
   with the kind permission of Bill Staines
Cover and interior design by Jim Brennan
Maps by Paperglyphs

Published by
Sono Nis Press
Box 160
Winlaw, BC V0G 2J0
1-800-370-5228

Distributed in the U.S. by
Orca Book Publishers
Box 468
Custer, WA 98240-0468
1-800-210-5277

books@sononis.com
www.sononis.com

Printed and bound in Canada by Kromar Printing.
Printed on acid-free paper that is forest friendly (100% post-consumer
recycled paper) and has been processed chlorine free.

For Annaliis and Stefan

≈

In memory of Mummu and Pappa,
with thankfulness for your gifts of Finnish heritage
and the spoon that sparked the idea for this story.

≈

S. D. G.

AUTHOR'S NOTE

This book is a work of fiction based on historical events. I have made every attempt to ensure historical accuracy. Any errors that remain are mine alone. All characters are fictional, except for the following, in order of reference or appearance: E. Pauline Johnson (Tekahionwake), Nellie McClung, Captain Henry George Kendall, Rudyard Kipling, Mabel Hackney, Laurence Irving, and Emmy the cat.

GLOSSARY

Juhannus	St. John's Day or Midsummer, a festival held on June 24 until 1955, when it was changed to the Saturday between June 20 and June 26
Kalevala	Finland's national epic poem, comprising the ancient songs of "rune singers"; these songs were collected by Elias Lönnrot and published in 1835
kantele	a traditional Finnish folk instrument, originally with five strings and resembling a lap harp or zither
kulta	gold
Mummu	grandma
näkkileipä	flat round rye bread, baked with a centre hole for threading onto a rod to dry, resulting in a thick crispbread
piirakka	small oval pie of rye crust filled with cooked rice and topped with a spread of hard-boiled egg and butter
pulla	sweet yeast bread flavoured with cardamom
sauna	Finnish steam bath
sisu	strength, drive, and perseverance

We are crossing the water our whole life through
We are making a passage that is straight and true
Every heart is a vessel, every dream is a light
Shining through the darkness of the blackest night

—BILL STAINES, "Crossing the Water"

"Mama, don't leave me."

The *Empress* listed. Panic shrank each breath.

"Papa, I need you," I moaned.

Far away a girl called, "Mom! Mummu's having a bad dream."

A gentle hand touched my shoulder. "Wake up. It's okay," said the girl. My upper body jerked and my eyelids fluttered.

She sat on the edge of my bed. "It's me. Aliisa. Do you want some water?"

My hands covered my face. "Icy water... pulling me down. The sound of... of..."

Startled by brisk footsteps, I looked up as a woman in jeans breezed into my bedroom. Who was she? Oh, yes, Susan. My granddaughter. Aliisa's mother.

"Thanks, honey," she said to Aliisa. Susan slid her arm under my shoulders to help me sit up. "Have a drink, Mummu."

I swallowed some water. How odd to have such a vivid dream during my afternoon nap. I held out my age-spotted hand, the skin shrink-wrapped over greenish-blue veins. Undeniable proof that I was no longer a child.

I put on my glasses, shed the multicoloured quilt, and eased my slippered feet to the floor. Susan supported my left side. I gripped my walker and slowly stood. Rolling it forward, I shuffled to the dresser. The upper drawer squeaked as I pulled the handle.

"This modern furniture always complains," I muttered, tugging harder. "If my husband had built it, the drawers would slide smoothly." I sighed heavily. "He had a magic touch with wood." I reached under the embroidered handkerchiefs for the small leather case. The brown leather was worn and splotchy, and tied around the middle was a fraying ribbon so faded it was barely blue.

Turning to Aliisa, I said, "Before I die, I want to—"

"You're not going to die for a long time, right?" Her sky-blue eyes grew enormous.

"Don't worry. I plan to stick around a few more years," I said, chuckling, "to see you light one hundred birthday candles without burning the house down." That coaxed a smile from her.

Lowering myself into the recliner, I held out the case and said, "I want you to have this."

Aliisa reached for the gift. "Thanks." She plopped to the floor, cross-legged, with a puzzled expression on her face. "What is it?"

What was she picturing? A string of pearls? A gold bracelet?

"Open it." I was certain I knew her well enough to predict she would cherish the contents.

Aliisa fumbled with the ribbon, working to untie the stubborn knot. Removing the lid, she unwrapped the cotton-batting cocoon to reveal the tarnished silver sugar spoon.

"Oh… it's, um… old."

Had I guessed wrong? She sounded so disappointed.

"Once it's polished it'll be quite beautiful," said her mother. "Mummu, is this the spoon you had on the *Empress of Ireland*?"

"Yes."

Aliisa ran a finger over the scalloped edges of the spoon's shallow bowl and the stemmed rose that formed the handle. She flipped it over and studied the tiny hallmark of the silversmith stamped into the back.

I stroked the length of her hair. "Satin-smooth and the colour of sunshine. Aliisa-*kulta*… have I told you my papa called me Saara-*kulta*?" I stared at my parents' wedding portrait on the bedside table. *It wasn't always golden between us, was it, Papa?*

My great-granddaughter clasped my gnarled hand and smiled briefly. "I really want to know what happened to you on that ship. Please tell me your *Empress* story, Mummu. The *whole* story."

I nodded, dabbing my eyes with a lilac-scented handkerchief. A few months after the *Empress* sank I had decided never to talk about it again. I had hoped that way my nightmares would stop. They did, until I read that anniversary article. Poking the newspaper beside me with its grainy photograph of the steamship *Empress of Ireland*, I said, "It's more real than ever. I can picture every detail of that huge ship." I could recall my early years better than what I had for dinner the night before.

11

"I'll try to tell you everything."

"I'd like to hear this, too," said Susan, making herself comfortable on the bed.

"Hmm… to tell the *whole* story," I began, arching my eyebrows at my audience, "I need to start several months before the trip, in December, 1913."

Aliisa settled into the old pine rocking chair.

"Christmas was lonely in Port Arthur. When Mama persuaded Papa to take us to Uncle's homestead in North Branch for New Year's, I nearly burst with excitement."

"How far away was it?" asked Aliisa. My stories usually made her think of questions. "How'd you get there?"

"Fourteen miles or so. Papa hired a horse and sleigh from the livery."

"What colour was the horse?"

"Aliisa, stop interrupting. Let Mummu talk."

Aliisa leaned back, shut her eyes, and rocked the chair on its extra-long runners. She cradled her silver spoon and listened to me tell my story.

"He was black as coal and spirited as the wind. 'Faster, Papa!' I'd say. My brother was nervous, but not me. What a thrilling ride. The cold air stung my face…"

Crack! Papa's whip snapped the coal-black horse. Chief snorted and plunged forward. The runners of the sleigh swished through the snowy ruts toward Auntie and Uncle's homestead in North Branch.

"Faster, Papa!" I said.

"Hang on tight, Saara!" He flapped the reins.

Cold wind stung my forehead but I grinned with delight. Frosted evergreens blurred as we flew past.

A quarter of a mile down the road Papa glanced back at me. "Fast enough for you, Saara?"

"Plenty fast," said John.

As Papa laughed and raised the whip again, one runner struck a high spot, slightly tilting the sleigh. John clutched the rail. "We're going to tip over!"

I glared at him. At eight, my brother shouldn't have been such a scaredy-cat anymore. I wanted so badly to say something mean to him. Not in Finnish, the language my family always used, but in English. Words formed in my head that I knew Mama wouldn't understand. Papa likely would, and I'd earn a scolding from him, so they stayed inside me to fester.

"Tauno, perhaps we should slow down," said Mama, reaching gloved hands to snug her fur hat over her ears.

Papa pulled the reins. The harness rattled, bells jangling, as the horse adjusted his pace to an easy trot. His heavy breathing produced clouds of steam around his nose and forelegs. I added my own steam with a gigantic sigh.

I scanned the snow for animal tracks. The bluish dotted lines punched into the white slopes reminded me of how the road would be drawn on a map. Imagining myself an eagle, I soared above my hometown, Port Arthur. There, below me, stood the castle-like grain elevators. They were planted along the shore of Lake Superior, guarding the hillside city. I swooped over the ice of Thunder Bay to the Sleeping Giant, the long, cliff-edged peninsula in the shape of an Indian brave lying on his back.

When the sun dipped behind a hill, the west wind made me shiver. Inside hand-knitted mittens, my icicle fingers curled stiffly around my thumbs. "I wish we lived closer to Auntie and Uncle."

"They won't move to the city," said Mama. "But if we bought land in North Branch…"

The words "I'd like that" were still a thought in my mind when Papa said, "Which we will never do." He gave Mama a hard look, his clean-shaven jaw rigid. "We belong in Port Arthur. Someday we'll buy our own house there."

I could once again hear Doris bragging on the last

day of school, "Now that we own a big house, all twenty-six relatives are coming for Christmas dinner." We had heaps of relatives, but not one had come to share the holiday with us. Everyone, except my aunt and uncle, lived half a world away, in Finland. I had never met my grandparents, my cousins, or anyone from there apart from Mama's sister Marja. To travel across the Atlantic Ocean filled my dreams.

Last winter, my parents had been a week away from buying steamship tickets when Aunt Marja and Arvo announced their summer wedding date. Then, in November, John had come down with pneumonia and some of the trip savings were gobbled up by doctor's bills. But ever since, Mama had been saving all of her earnings from sewing. Her little sister Aili would be married at Juhannus in June. Mama wanted her whole family to be at the wedding even though the trip would cost over four hundred dollars.

As we drew close to North Branch I pictured the farmhouse the next night packed with guests for the New Year's Eve party. Aunt Marja's invitation had said, "*The celebration will crown the year past and joyfully anticipate the future.*"

"Mama," I said, crossing my fingers.

"What is it?"

"I hope *this* is the year we go to Finland!"

Papa turned to Mama and frowned. "Have you been making promises? We may not be able to spare the money."

"But, Tauno," said Mama, "the wedding..."

15

I couldn't understand the expression on Papa's face, but I wondered what could be more important than our trip.

Twilight's yellow horizon framed the barn, outbuildings, and farmhouse when we arrived. Snow draped from each roof edge like a blanket sliding off a bed. Before the sleigh stopped, the door of the moss-chinked log house swung open.

"Hello," called Uncle Arvo, pulling on his coat. "Come inside and thaw out. I'll tend to the horse."

I hopped down and patted Chief's warm, damp neck. He smelled of sweat. A haze of steam rose from his shaggy back. We filed along the trampled path to where Aunt Marja stood in the doorway, her arms spread wide. The delicious aroma of beef stew drifted from the kitchen.

"Emilia, how wonderful to see you." She embraced her sister. "Welcome, Tauno. Jussi, you've certainly grown." She ruffled John's light brown hair. "And Saara…" I rushed into her arms. The words whispered into my ear alone made me blush. "…I saved the best for last." Holding me at arm's length, she stroked my hair. "Satin-smooth and the colour of sunshine. Such a beautiful young lady." I laughed to myself. Me, beautiful?

That evening, my happiness swelled when Papa raved about my brilliant poetry recitation at the school Christmas concert. Like embers in a wood stove, I glowed inside when I blew out the coal oil lamp and crawled beneath the patchwork quilt at bedtime.

Early the next morning, air cold enough to freeze nose hairs blasted Aunt Marja and me when we stepped outside to fetch split birch logs from the woodpile. Bands of pale orange and pink stretched across the sky behind the grove of naked birch trees. The snow squeaked underfoot as we tramped back to the house. Inside, the scent of frothing yeast for *pulla* dough filled the room. Auntie removed her coat and tied on her flour-sack apron. She'd grown rounder in front. My baby cousin would be born when the lilacs bloomed.

Steam was rising from a large pot on the stove. Mama stirred oats into the boiling water. Aunt Marja began slicing a loaf of rye bread and said, "Saara, would you set the table for me, please?"

I cringed at how she pronounced my name: "Sawra." "Could you say 'Sarah'? That's what I'm called at school." Mama shook her head. I had given up trying to persuade my parents.

"You don't like your Finnish name?" asked Auntie.

"Yes... I mean, no," I said, my cheeks growing warm. "I prefer the Canadian way."

"When an Englishman says Marja it sounds awful." She and I giggled. Why was it so difficult for them to remember to say the *j* like a *y*?

"Are the Koskis coming to the party tonight?" I asked, setting out cups and spoons.

"Yes, and the rest of the neighbours as well."

I'd met eleven-year-old Lila Koski the previous summer while staying with Auntie and Uncle. When Lila and I had finished our morning chores, we would explore the forest and often swim in the Koskis' tiny lake.

Mama ladled the steaming cereal into bowls. Aunt Marja set one at each place as John and the men returned

17

from the barn.

"Thank you for taking over my barn chores this morning," said Auntie.

"You're welcome," said Uncle Arvo, rubbing his chapped hands on his woollen mackinaw pants. He sat down and wrapped his fingers around his dish. "That feels better."

Papa harrumphed. "The only good thing about farming in this miserable cold is having no mosquitoes." He smoothed his rumpled dark brown hair from the side part downward. My hunger turned to dread. Our last visit had ended with him and Uncle loudly comparing city life and homesteading. To me, it sounded like arguing, but Mama called it "discussing."

Uncle raised his eyebrows, his mouth twitching as if to grin. He bowed his head and said grace. After Auntie poured the coffee, she perched on the stool by the wood stove.

"Jussi," said Uncle, "after breakfast you can set the ice lanterns along the path." John nodded, his mouth full. "Then you can work with us men again." My brother looked ridiculous smiling with dribbles of milk on his chin.

Papa frowned, making his moustache droop. "I planned to read my Finnish newspapers, but if you really need me—"

"I could take your place," I blurted. Chopping kindling, or even shovelling manure, was better than any job in the kitchen.

"Of course not, Saara," said Papa. "Girls belong inside."

I slumped on the bench. He didn't approve of my handling an axe or the workhorses, claiming it was too dangerous. But I'd had more injuries in a kitchen than a barn. The more careful I aimed to be doing inside chores, the more awkwardly I behaved. Mama had attempted to teach me to knit countless times without success, yet I'd swiftly learned to harness Uncle's workhorses.

John nudged my foot under the table and faked a look of sympathy. I wished for the six hundredth time I'd been born a boy. My brother never did kitchen work.

"I do need your help today, Saara."

"Yes, Auntie."

"And when the time comes, you can braid the *pulla*." She knew handling the warm stretchy dough with its cardamom scent was the one task I enjoyed.

On his way outdoors with the men, John smirked. I stuck out my tongue at him and grabbed a woven basket to carry potatoes from the root house built into the hill. I dawdled coming back, watching a chickadee who "dee-deed" from a nearby balsam. Uncle carried freshly cut evergreen boughs across the yard and dumped them by the door of the house.

"Uncle, don't forget about the predictions tonight."

"I don't need molten lead to tell me you're going to Finland. Your mother won't miss Aili's wedding for anything." He winked. "But I won't forget."

The kitchen buzzed with activity. Raw onion fumes overpowered the yeast scent. I set the basket of potatoes on the floor near Mama, who was peeling turnips over the slop pail. Grabbing a knife and the biggest potato, I sat beside her.

"*Oma tupa, oma lupa,*" said Mama.

Her poetic phrase intrigued me. "I'm not sure what that saying means."

"'When one owns his own place, he is his own boss.'" Mama sighed and looked at her sister. "I wish Tauno would come to his senses and buy farmland instead of renting a city house. We do save some money out of his pay packet from the lumber mill every week, but our backyard is hardly worth gardening."

"What if we got a cow instead of growing vegetables?" I asked, dropping the skinned potato in the bowl of water and rubbing my itchy nose with my earth-scented hand.

Mama shook her head. "Then we must pay a man to take her to pasture every day. No, as we say in the Old Country, 'we live as we can, not as we may wish.'" I wrinkled my still-itchy nose and wished that Mama wouldn't always be so sensible. The fire popped and crackled in the stove.

"Emilia, your husband is a hard worker." Auntie finished shaping meatballs and washed her hands. "And as long as we have a farm, you won't starve. Although you may get sick of potatoes and turnips."

At the window, she craned her neck, inspecting the small building nearby. "Is that smoke from the chimney? Yes. Arvo remembered to heat the sauna. Ahh... the steam will feel so good. I can wash away the smell of onions, clean to greet the New Year." She stretched her arms. "I wonder what nineteen hundred and fourteen will bring our way?"

"Will you be coming to Finland with us for the wedding?" I asked. Mama frowned, so I added, "If we go, that is."

"I..." Auntie began, then slowly sat at the table.

"I'm sorry. I forgot about the baby."

Mama signalled for me to hush.

Aunt Marja picked up her silver sugar spoon. "Mother's fare-thee-well gift." She traced the rose, leaves, and stem that formed the spoon's handle. "To remind me I'm as sweet as sugar to her. I kept this spoon in my handbag, Saara, when my first husband and I sailed on the *Titanic*. Everyone said the ship was unsinkable. But..." She wiped away a tear with her apron. "Now I get nervous in a rowboat on a pond, for heaven's sake."

How terrible to fear going on a ship. For me, it would be a dream come true.

"Enough talk about boats and trips," said Mama. "There's a party tonight and plenty of work left to do."

By sunset, the festive table was ready. The candles I had set in wooden holders stood in the middle of the linen tablecloth, surrounded by beet salad, raspberry preserves, and loaves of rye bread and cardamom-scented *pulla*.

After Mama, Auntie, and I took our turn in the sauna, I put on my green Sunday dress and Mama tied matching ribbons near the ends of my two thick braids. Mama and Auntie both wore their light brown hair swept up into a bun. I watched out the window for Lila. The ice lanterns made a cheery pathway through the snow. Before long, the silhouettes of skiers appeared. The Koski family and their hired men removed their skis, planting them tips up in the snow, then stomped their boots on the branch-mat before entering.

Once the Seppäläs and Lehtos arrived, Uncle Arvo said grace. Aunt Marja announced, "Everyone help yourselves while the food is hot."

Lila and I claimed two stools in a corner, our plates heaping. She chuckled. "Look at us—we could pass as twins with our long blond hair and blue eyes, and both being tall for eleven."

Between mouthfuls of *piirakka* and meatballs I told her about the recent school concert, and then described what had happened when a boarder from eastern Europe came to my best friend Helena's house. "It was Christmas Eve. Helena's mother was so busy she forgot to explain the sauna to him before he went to get cleaned up. From the backyard we heard him yelling. He had emptied half a bucket of water over the heated rocks on the stove."

Pretending my stool was the sauna stove, I mimed upending a pail. I coughed and struggled to breathe in the thick steam. Stooping, I groped for the door and backed into the "red-hot stove," knocking over my stool. Lila gasped.

"He scorched his hand on the doorknob getting out and shouted a flurry of words. The only English ones were curses." We laughed so hard our eyes watered.

The sound of a violin being tuned interrupted us. Uncle Arvo rolled up the woven rag mats, revealing the smooth jack pine floor. The table, chairs, and benches were pushed against the walls. Mrs. Seppälä strummed her *kantele* and one of the hired men warmed up his mouth organ. It was time to dance.

"Tauno," said Uncle Arvo, "who can last the longest?"

"There's no contest," bantered Papa, smiling.

They drew their wives into the centre of the room. The ladies' long dresses billowed as their partners whirled them around in time with the lively tunes. Lila and I joined in. Our not-quite-so-long dresses flared, while our braids took flight. Even the boys danced. Lila's cheeks soon matched her red woollen dress. If Auntie hadn't been expecting and feeling extra tired, she and Uncle would have outlasted even my parents. Mrs. Seppälä led us in singing two Finnish folk songs. Then Papa stood tall, becoming the storyteller of the ancient Kalevala. With a commanding presence, he spun a tale of struggle between good and evil. Nature sprang to life in the word pictures he painted.

"Saara-*kulta*," he called. Saara-gold. His special name for me.

"Yes, Papa?"

"As one of the next generation of poetry reciters, will you present 'The Sleeping Giant'?"

My school concert piece—he wanted everyone to hear it. A thrill poured over me. I breathed deeply and closed my eyes to focus on Pauline Johnson's poem about the local rock formation. "*When did you sink to your dreamless sleep, out there in your thunder bed?*" I began. By the time I finished the fourth verse I felt weightless, soaring on winds of applause, both past and present. I sought out Auntie's eyes. She dabbed them with her handkerchief. Papa clapped the longest, as he had at the Christmas concert.

Midnight arrived. We toasted a welcome to the coming year.

Uncle Arvo said, "Who's ready for a prediction?" I chewed the end of one braid, waiting for someone else to go first. Mr. Koski stepped forward. Uncle melted a small piece of lead and plunged it into cold water to harden. I pressed closer to see what shape it had formed.

"A fortunate year for you, Eino. See the bulges? There's money coming your way."

For Aunt Marja the molten lead also revealed bumps. "Maybe that's not for wealth," said Mr. Lehto, "but for a big, healthy baby boy." He nudged Uncle Arvo.

I gulped. "May I have a turn?"

The metal hissed and sputtered when Uncle dropped it into the water. "That looks like a boat to me."

My heart skipped.

With a broad smile he said, "Saara, this will be a travelling year for you." He spoke with such certainty, it *had* to be true. I would finally meet my grandparents!

"Arvo, why do you bother with this nonsense? Only fools take this seriously," said Papa, scowling, his bushy eyebrows almost meeting. "Some Old Country traditions have no place here in Canada."

How I wanted to believe my fortune was true. But Papa had spoiled it.

Uncle studied the tiny ship. "Black spots…"

"What do they mean?" I asked.

"They are a sign of sadness, but no need to fret. They're small and few."

24

2

Late afternoon on New Year's Day we reached the outskirts of Port Arthur. A straight column of woodsmoke rose from every chimney. John napped and I pretended to be asleep, all the while thinking about my uncle's prediction. He had sounded convinced at the party and again in the morning when we harnessed Chief. For Uncle Arvo, the fortunes had always come true. What if he was right?

Papa guided Chief up Foley Street and onto the lane where our two-storey house stood with only two others. We unloaded the baskets of potatoes and turnips and carted them through the enclosed porch, down the hall, and into the kitchen. Leaving Mama to store them in the basement cold cellar, Papa and I drove the sleigh back to the Star Livery. I hugged Chief's bushy neck as I whispered farewell.

We walked briskly along Bay Street from one circle of street-lamp light to the next. I stretched my scarf up to cover my nose so my breath could warm my chin.

"In three weeks the library at the Big Finn Hall should

receive a large order of books from Finland," said Papa. "I volunteered to organize them."

"May a hepp?" The scarf muffled my words.

Papa laughed. "Would you like to help me?"

I yanked my scarf down to say, "Oh, yes!"

It was good to have something to look forward to, as January settled in. John missed the first week of school because of a nasty cold. One day in mid-January, after Helena and I struggled home from school in a near blizzard, Mama had me deliver a package to one of her customers. Back at home, I tossed my coat on a hook in the porch, removed my rubber overshoes, and flung open the front door. "Mama!"

The stench of boiling turnips met me as I dashed into the kitchen and pulled two fifty-cent pieces from my mitten. "Look! Mrs. Hopkins gave me more money than you told me to charge her for the blouse."

Mama beamed, accepted the coins, and deposited them in her coffee-tin bank.

"She said she's never seen such perfect stitching by a seamstress." Sipu purred and pressed her grey cheek against my leg. I scooped her up for a cuddle before washing my hands. I began setting the white enamel-topped kitchen table. "She is recommending you to all her friends. We'll have our fares paid in no time!"

"It is good to live in hope," said Mama, mashing the turnips. "Only three plates, Saara. Papa has a labour meeting right after work."

"Again?" I sighed.

"Being the labour spokesman he must present the

workers' concerns to the company. Therefore he needs to hear them out."

"Will he be home before I go to bed?"

"He will be home when he's home."

Later, as faint light from street lamps filtered through my curtains, I lay in bed wishing that Papa would return before I fell asleep. I thought about the night of the school Christmas concert. He had been so proud of my recitation, and when he came to my bedroom to say goodnight he sang his "Saara song":

Minä pikku tytölleni
univirren laulan;
Pane pikku simmu kiinni
ja nuku Herran rauhaan.

To my little girl
I will sing a bedtime prayer;
Close your little eyes
and sleep in God's peace.

I had felt treasured for many days afterward. Papa had bragged, to whoever would listen, of his "brilliant Saara." But he hadn't sung my song to me since.

At last, the books for the library arrived. After supper on the following Saturday, Papa and I climbed the stairs to the second floor of the Finnish Labour Temple—the Big Finn Hall. There, stacked on a long wooden table, were at least fifty volumes.

27

"Golly!" Caressing their smooth covers, I breathed in the scent of paper, ink, and glue.

"To begin with we'll sort them into non-fiction and fiction," said Papa. Winking, he added, "No reading until we're done organizing."

"I can wait." I chuckled. "But can you?"

His blue eyes danced at my challenge and we launched into our task. When we were done, Papa pulled out his pocket watch and I was shocked at the late hour. We hurried home. I had unfinished chores, but he sent me straight to bed.

Waking up the next morning, I felt oddly warm. For the last Sunday in January, it was unusually mild. Downstairs, Papa sat hunched over the kitchen table, rubbing his eyes.

Mama poured coffee into a cup and set it in front of him. "Perhaps you should stay home from gymnastic club practice this morning and catch up on the sleep you missed stewing about work overnight."

About to tell Papa how much I'd enjoyed helping him in the library, I tripped on my bootlace and stumbled into my chair.

"Quiet, child!" He groaned, holding his head in his hands. "Tie your laces before you break your neck."

Blushing, I did as I was told, then fetched a bottle of milk from the icebox, brown sugar from the cupboard, and spoons from the drawer, placing them gently on the table.

"Tauno," said Mama, "there is nothing you can do

about the situation until you meet with the company."

John clattered down the stairs, but Papa made no comment. How unfair. Papa never lectured my brother.

Mama stirred the porridge and said, "Saara, I need more wood."

"You forgot to refill the woodbox again?" snapped Papa, his eyes an angry red. "You know you are responsible for doing that before you go to bed."

"Yes, Papa." I sped to the woodpile. Had he forgotten he had told me to leave the chore undone the night before?

Over breakfast I managed to draw no further attention to myself.

As Mama handed John his coat, he said, "I don't want to go to church. I want to watch Papa's gymnastics practice."

"You must go to church," said Mama.

"But Papa hasn't gone since Christmas."

Mama frowned. "Tauno, couldn't you come with us to church and then go to the practice? It runs until two o'clock, doesn't it?"

"If I did that I would miss the group practice," said Papa. "I like to get there early so I can be home for Sunday lunch. You do want me here for that, don't you?"

"Yes, that is true. But I also want you at church."

Papa shrugged and turned to John. "Next Sunday I will stay later and you can come to watch on your way home from church, all right?"

John's face lit up with a huge smile. "Hurrah!"

Mama, John, and I walked to church—the Finnish

Lutheran Church on Wilson Street—marvelling at the spring-like temperature. After the service and the reading of the announcements, I hurried outside to face the sun and soak up its warmth while I waited for Mama to finish visiting.

On our way home, Mama strode well ahead, holding her long skirt above her ankles, clear of the mud. John dawdled behind me, stomping in the slush. Soon Mama disappeared around the corner at Secord Street.

Splash. John launched rock after rock into a puddle on a vacant lot. Mucky water splattered his boots, socks, and tweed knickers. If Mama were here she'd have hauled him away.

I heard a bark. Loping toward John was a shaggy mud-covered dog, his tail winding around his rump like a propeller. He planted his dripping paws on my brother's chest, knocking him backwards. The mutt's slobbery tongue licked John's entire face as he hollered, "Get off! Help!"

"He's only saying hello, you scaredy-cat." John would be scolded for getting his Sunday clothes dirty. Served him right. I snickered and marched uphill, narrowly missing a steaming pile of horse manure.

John screamed.

I whipped around and froze, holding my breath. The animal had pinned my little brother to the ground, tail wagging, but jaws clamped around his arm. I checked over my shoulder to see if Mama was coming to his rescue, but she was nowhere in sight.

John screamed again. "Help me, Saara!"

I charged toward them, yelling, "Get out of here!" Grabbing a stick, I whacked the dog's back. He yelped and scrambled off, tail between his legs.

John wailed and rolled on his side, clutching his arm. I threw the stick after the dog.

"I'm going to bleed to death!"

"Let me see your arm." He sat up and sobbed as I folded back his sleeve. "There's no blood, John."

"Why did he bite me?"

"The dog was only playing. He didn't mean to hurt you." Hugging my frightened brother, I rocked him. My heart pumped wildly. "You're safe now."

Once his trembling passed, I retrieved his sopping cap and we walked hand in hand the rest of the way home.

"Jussi, your clothes are filthy," said Mama. "Saara, your dress—"

John snivelled, holding his arm. "A dog attacked me."

Mama inhaled sharply.

"Saara scared him away."

Papa flung down his newspaper and rushed over to inspect John's arm. "Whose dog was it?" he demanded.

"I've never seen it before," I said.

Papa patted John on the back. "No need for a doctor, Jussi, but there will be a large bruise."

"I should not have gone ahead," said Mama. "Thank goodness Saara was with you." She filled the copper boiler with cold water to soak our mud-drenched clothes overnight. After changing, I read in the parlour while John bathed in the washtub on the kitchen floor. Papa tucked my shaken, but clean, brother in bed for a rest.

That's when the scolding came. Papa stormed into the parlour. "Saara, you should have helped Jussi sooner! He could have been seriously hurt by that dog."

My cheeks flushed. "The dog was friendly—"

"Nonsense. A friendly dog doesn't growl and charge."

"He was playful—"

Papa's eyebrows furrowed and he shook his head. I wanted to tell him the dog was wagging his tail, but there was no point in trying to convince Papa. He always believed John over me.

"Jussi said the dog held him down and you walked away," shouted Papa. "How could you leave him?"

"I... I did my best."

"You ought to know better. I expect you to watch out for your brother. You will spend the rest of today in your room. But first, get the switch."

Banished to my room, the backs of my legs smarting from their beating, my stomach squirmed with guilt. The truth was, I had wanted my brother to get into trouble. I shuddered, imagining how much worse it could have been for John if the dog *had* meant to hurt him.

During the next two weeks icy north winds returned and Mama steadily added to her coffee-tin bank. One evening I peeked into the tin and gasped. "Where is all the money?"

"Don't worry, Saara," said Mama. "I deposited it in the Royal Bank. At the rate I'm saving, by Easter we may have enough for the trip."

Papa slammed his fist on the table so hard the cups and saucers rattled. "There will be no travelling if I must go on strike."

"Strike?" said Mama, her hand flying to her throat. "Has it come to that?"

"No one has yet uttered the word, but it's what I expect."

"Oh, Tauno…"

Once the kitchen was tidy, Mama transferred the ground coffee from its tin into a quart sealer. She washed and dried the tin before placing it in front of the trip savings tin in the cupboard.

"What's that for?" I asked.

"In case of a strike. Tomorrow's supper will be rice pudding on its own."

I silently prayed, "Please let there be no strike." I wasn't sure exactly what a strike was, but it worried Mama.

By the end of February it felt as if I had no father, and I had learned what "strike" meant: Papa would refuse to work until the situation was resolved, and he would have no income, perhaps for many weeks. Mama served rice pudding for supper once a week. All of her earnings were stored in the Strike Fund tin. Papa attended meetings every night. He came home angry after every one, it seemed. *Bang!* The slamming door would jolt me awake, heart racing. Papa's loud voice would boom through the kitchen, pouring up the heating pipes and into my bedroom. "Fools! Can't they see? The only way to improve our working conditions is to go on strike."

Fear twisted my stomach. It sounded as if Papa *wanted* a strike. What would we have to do without if he wasn't working? I reached for Sipu, curled at the foot of my bed, and cradled her purring warmth under the covers. The wool blankets scratched my face, so I snuggled underneath the flannelette sheet and prayed that sleep would take me away.

I spent as much time as I could with my best friend, Helena Pekkonen. After school, if Mama had no errands for me to run and my chores were done, I headed down the steep back lane to Helena's house. She had been my best friend since she'd arrived from Finland seven years before. She was in my class, though she was a year older than I was.

One afternoon, after my share of the ironing was done, I left to play with Helena. At the rear of the Pekkonens' boarding house I opened the door and walked through the porch to knock on the inner door. Helena appeared, her dark blond hair in two braids identical to mine, apart from the ribbons she always wore.

"Do you have time for a game of Parcheesi?" I asked, shedding my coat.

"Yes, after I change Mandi's diaper *and* rock her to sleep *and* finish the ironing."

"I'll gladly take care of Mandi."

"Thank you." She smiled. "I'll be red, okay?"

Once Helena's baby sister was tucked in her wicker carriage outside for her daily fresh-air nap, I set up the board game in the parlour. We took turns rolling the dice, trying for a five.

"What is the name of the boat you came on when you immigrated?"

"Oh, the *Empress of Ireland*. One of Canadian Pacific's grand steamships." Helena dropped the dice she'd been holding. "When your family goes to Finland you should try to book passage on that ship. The stewards treated us so kindly, especially when we all got seasick."

"Ugh!" I grimaced and rolled the dice again. "Hurrah, a five at last!"

Later, when all four of my markers were finally in play, Mrs. Pekkonen poked her head into the room to say it was time for Helena to set the tables for supper. At home, I was surprised to find Papa already there, deep in a "discussion" with Mama in the parlour. John sat at the kitchen table, eating freshly baked cardamom cookies.

"Tauno, couldn't you try one more time to talk with the company?"

"I've talked long and hard," spouted Papa, "but they remain totally unfair."

"Can I have your share?" asked John, his mouth full.

I shook my head and shushed John. Snatching two cookies, I listened at the parlour door. My heart beat as fast as trotting hooves. What had happened at the lumber mill?

"No wage increase whatsoever!" I could hear Papa pacing. "The workers say it is time for action. One man dared to bring his gun to the meeting."

Papa could be in danger!

"I want to know what kind of gun he had," said John, heading toward the parlour.

"No!" I whispered, grabbing the back of his shirt. "Stay here."

"You must do everything you can to avoid violence," said Mama. "There have been too many injuries and deaths in this city over strikes."

"I will do my best, Emilia. We strike tomorrow."

No travelling if I go on strike, Papa had said. The sweet cookie in my mouth turned tasteless.

Once the strike began, Papa was home more, but it wasn't pleasant to have him there. I stayed out of his way to avoid his barking. One more "This is a meal, Saara, not a race," or "Wash those dishes again, they're still greasy," and I would surely scream.

As soon as I finished my Saturday chores and my composition for school, and before Papa could get home from picketing, I left for Helena's house. I took the long way, across Banning Street and down the Bay Street hill.

Mrs. Pekkonen sent me upstairs to Helena's bedroom. She lay on her bed, drumming her pencil on her open composition book, the page blank except for a title.

"Saara—you rescued me from torture!" Helena dropped her pencil and grabbed a deck of cards from her dresser. "How about a game of All-Fours?"

Nodding, I sat cross-legged on the woven rag mat. We played several rounds with intense concentration.

Throughout the next round, I chewed the tip of one braid. I played my last card. Helena tallied the points.

"Forty-nine, I win," she said. "What's wrong? You don't usually let me win."

"It's this horrid strike. Over two weeks already," I said, folding my arms across my chest. "My father's always in a bad mood."

"At least he's in Port Arthur. My father's been at the lumber camp so long I forget what he looks like." Helena gathered the cards into a tidy stack. "I'm certain the strike will end soon." She spent a long time shuffling the deck. "How about you *try* to beat me this time?"

"You think I've lost my touch? Deal." I flashed a grin her way as I flipped my braids onto my back. We played card games until Baby Mandi woke from her nap and wailed. It was time for Helena to return to her duties. Plodding up the snowy lane toward home, I made a fervent wish for the strike to be over.

On Monday, as I set the kitchen table, John breezed in from outside. His cheeks and nose were bright red and bits of snow clung to his brown wool knickers and thick socks. He sniffed the air. "What's for supper?"

"Beef stew and dumplings," said Mama. "Mrs. Brooks paid me in meat for the dress I sewed." Sipu purred, rubbing against my legs. I scratched behind her grey velvet ears.

Hearing Papa enter the house gave me a sinking feeling. The food didn't smell or look so wonderful anymore. He approached the table in silence, then astounded me by producing Cocoa Dips and caramels for us from his trousers pocket. He tousled John's hair, then mine, freeing the shorter strands from my braids.

Papa sat on the edge of his chair. "So far, we Finns alone have risked going on strike. Today that changed." His blue eyes shone. "The Hungarians have joined our cause."

Pouring from the full bottle of milk, I dripped some on the table. I focused on my stew, expecting Papa to lecture me. But he kept talking, ignoring my clumsiness.

"The strike will not last much longer."

Mama placed her hand on his. "That is wonderful news."

"Once I'm back to work we can start saving again. By

next year we will have our down payment for a house. No more renting."

A house? But what about the trip?

Five days later Papa came home only half an hour after leaving for picket duty, and panic gripped my throat. I had never seen my father so downcast. Mama sat him at the kitchen table and poured strong coffee. The strike had ended, not because the workers had won, but because they had all been fired.

Papa's dark-rimmed eyes stared into his cup. "It shouldn't have turned out this way." He shook his head. "The strike was supposed to get us more pay, not cost us our jobs."

Mama whisked me and John into the parlour. "Let's leave Papa alone. Now don't you two worry, we have enough savings to last awhile." She spoke quickly, her hands wringing her apron. "Papa will find another job soon, and I will take in more sewing."

I knew her words were meant to comfort us, but my snarling fears wouldn't budge. When Mama fished money out of the Strike Fund and asked us to buy eggs and butter, I felt a pang of sorrow. Every coin removed meant going backward in our trip saving, and it was already the third week of March. How could I keep my dream alive?

About an hour after lunch, the strike committee arrived. I helped Mama serve coffee. Answering another knock on the front door, I found Helena. The falling snow had whitened her hat, coat, and braids.

"Aren't you coming over this afternoon?" she asked.

"I forgot." My voice sounded flat, lifeless. Stepping into the porch, I closed the inner door behind me. "Helena, my father lost his job. The strike committee's having coffee in the parlour. It's like a funeral in there."

"What will happen? Do you have to move out?"

"No, I don't think so." Icy air slipped through my coarse cotton sleeves, turning my arms to gooseflesh. "But it's up to me to earn some money or we'll never get to Finland. Maybe I can clean stalls at the Star Livery."

"Only if you dressed in knickers and tucked your braids under a cap." Helena snickered. "Imagine that."

"How can you laugh about this? It's serious." But despite the cold that numbed my face, I couldn't help smiling for the first time that day.

4

Unseasonably warm weather greeted us a few days later. I slammed the porch door and stepped square in a puddle. "Arrrg." In my haste I'd forgotten my rubber overshoes. I huffed my way down the back lane.

"Wait for me," called John. He normally walked to school with the neighbour boy, Fred, but that morning Fred had to have a tooth pulled. Papa had made it clear I was responsible for my brother getting to school safely, but I carried on. I was in no mood for his babbling. Wasn't he old enough to look after himself?

Passing Helena's house, I sighed. It was bound to be a dreary day without her. She had felt feverish the day before so her mother insisted she stay home. I prayed it wasn't serious. Last week the seven-year-old McTavish boy had died of scarlet fever. His family's house was a block up the hill. I shivered.

Turning, I motioned for my brother to walk faster. "We should hurry, John."

He was unusually quiet. Kivelä Bakery's heavenly

aroma reached us at Secord Street. The tempting smell of yeast bread brought no comfort. It reminded me of our kitchen and my parents' stomach-churning quarrel at the breakfast table. They had never argued right in front of us before. Papa had ranted over lack of money, lack of jobs, and no lack of new immigrants to compete for the little work available.

"They keep coming. The employment lines get longer."

"Tauno, we should talk about this after the children go to school," said Mama, but he wouldn't quit.

"Single men get work before me. They have no families to support. How can you stand to help the immigrants? To *welcome* them?" Mama and other church ladies visited new immigrants from Finland, bringing them basic supplies like potatoes, sugar, and coffee. "You care more for people fresh from the Old Country than your own family."

His words were like a blow without a fist attached. Mama's face paled, but she kept her voice level. "We have a home and enough food and clothes. Yes, I want a steady job for you. But as long as God provides what we need to live I will keep helping newcomers. Have you forgotten how lost we were in the beginning?" My parents often spoke of their long journey in 1900 from Finland to the "Promised Land." Canada offered wealth to those willing to work hard, Papa had said.

Whack! Something struck me between the shoulder blades.

"Morning, Miss Hill. Or is it Miss *Mountain*?" taunted Richard. Running along the path from his porch to the street he smoothed a snowball in his hands. He never let me forget the day in Junior First when I told the teacher my surname was "Hill" instead of "Mäki." I was so proud of my Finnish-English translation.

I dropped my books. "I'm going to get you."

"We'll be late," said John.

"Go on. I'll catch up."

Scooping a mittful of snow, I packed it together and hurled it at Richard. When it hit his knee instead of his grin, I knew I was in trouble.

"That's your best shot?" He splattered my wool coat three times before I could get another snowball in the air.

As he closed in, my aim improved. Hitting Richard on the neck twisted his mouth into a sneer. He sprang forward, pulled me down, and washed my face with snow. I spat out gritty slush, using my bare hand to shave snow from my cheeks.

The South Ward Public School bell rang. With my forehead stinging from the scrape of ice crystals, I plucked my belongings from the snowbank and sprinted to Cornwall Avenue. I *had* to reach my class before opening exercises. Breathing heavily, I entered the brick building and climbed upstairs to the Senior Third classroom. The final lines of "God Save the King" were being sung as I dumped my coat, mittens, hat, and scarf in the cloakroom that reeked of wet wool. I tried to slip into my fifth-row desk unnoticed.

It was not my lucky day.

After reading the morning Scriptures, Mr. McKee

said, "Saara, report your tardiness to the office."

"Yes, sir." There went my perfect attendance record.

When I returned, the pupils were copying arithmetic problems from the blackboard. "Drat," I said under my breath. I wouldn't finish the sums in time, no matter how fast I worked. As expected, I had to keep working at my desk during recess.

Once the students were back in the classroom, Mr. McKee announced a spelling match. My spine tingled at the challenge. "The captains are Robert and Saara." We positioned ourselves on opposite sides of the classroom. "Ladies first."

"I choose Helena... I mean... Doris."

"William," said Robert.

The selecting continued until the desks were emptied and two lines of students stood facing each other across the room. I was given the first word.

"School."

"S-c-h-o-o-l, school."

To Robert, Mr. McKee gave "February." With a slight hesitation, he spelled the word correctly.

The match carried on for several minutes. The word "rhythm" stumped Doris and she was eliminated. Richard, on Robert's team, tried the tough word, succeeded, and smirked at me. The teams shrank as the words became more difficult. Finally, I stood alone.

Mr. McKee assigned "immigrant" to Mary, one of three pupils left on Robert's side. I didn't hear her response. All I could think of was Papa's ugly accusation at breakfast.

My teacher gave the next word.

Everyone stared at me, waiting for me to speak.

"O-x-e-n, oxen."

Laughter burst out in the suspense-filled room. My cheeks flared. Someone whispered, "Oxygen, not oxen." Gloating, Robert gave the correct spelling.

Darting to my seat, I felt like a new immigrant with not one friendly soul in my entire world. I slumped onto my desk, burying my face in my arms to hide the embarrassing tears. It was all Papa's fault.

The sting of humiliation from my worst-ever spelling performance faded slowly, without Helena to help it go away. She did not have a serious illness—only a mild influenza—but she missed four days of school. On the day she returned, she needed my help to cart home her stack of school work. There was no point in asking her to play. I found Mama at her sewing machine trimming the seams of a blouse.

"Hello, Saara. Pastor Hannunen wants you to meet someone at the Immigration Hall tomorrow."

"Who?"

"A girl your age." Mama looked up from picking bits of white thread from her navy blue skirt. "Senja and her family arrived from Finland today. She has no English, so he would like you and Helena to help her find her way."

"All right." I could learn more about Finland from Senja.

Mama slowly shook her head. "I will never forget my first days in Port Arthur. We knew no one."

Before she could reminisce further, I asked if I could go and tell Helena.

"You may, but be home in time to help prepare supper."

Helena stood outside her back door removing snow-covered frozen diapers from the clothesline. She waved and held one finger to her lips. Mandi lay snugly wrapped in the carriage having her nap.

I signalled for Helena to come down the rickety wooden steps. Once she heard about the arrangement, she was keen to meet Senja. "There's so much to teach her. Remember me as a scared-stiff six-year-old who could only say hello and bye-bye? What would I have done without you?" Helena put her arm around me and squeezed hard. "I wish we could play Parcheesi, but I had better start my homework."

In the morning, as we passed Richard's house, he bellowed, "Hey, Miss Hill. Need any *oxygen* on your mountain?"

I blushed and Helena pulled on my hand. "Come on, let's beat him to school."

An undercurrent of excitement coloured our ordinary day. At dismissal, Helena and I raced outside. We chattered and giggled non-stop along the route to our church to meet Pastor Hannunen.

He greeted us, smiling. "You will make a young lady happy today."

Walking alongside him, we said little. Up ahead, on a vacant lot, several older boys were carrying on a frenzied snowball fight. They shifted closer and closer to the street. One snowball missed its target and slammed into the flank of a dappled grey horse pulling a sleigh. The horse screamed and reared. His driver struggled to keep him from bolting, meanwhile filling the air with cursing. The pastor quickened our pace.

Finally the stark white walls of the Immigration Hall stood before us. Inside, Pastor Hannunen introduced us to the Kallio family: Senja, her older brother, and her parents.

"Pleased to meet you," I said, offering my right hand.

"Welcome to Canada, Senja," said Helena. "We can show you around and teach you English."

"Helena," said Pastor Hannunen, "you and Senja will see a lot of each other. The Kallios are moving into your family's boarding house tomorrow." He and Mr. Kallio arranged the details of transporting their large trunk and other belongings.

Senja wrinkled her nose and said, "This place is horrible! In Helsinki we lived in a lovely apartment building."

I shrugged. "It's better than the shacks some people live—"

Senja cut me off. "Helena, tell me about your house."

"Oh, it's much prettier. There—"

"I'm certain it's splendid," she said, studying Helena from head to toe. "I can tell you come from a respectable family."

I stared at the smudge of pencil lead on my creased dress. My boots were scuffed and several strands of hair, loosened from my braids, dangled in my face. Senja looked at me and turned up her nose.

To Helena, she said, "I'll be fourteen soon. How old are you?"

"Thirteen and Saara is—"

"Almost twelve," I said.

"We go to South Ward Public School," chirped Helena, "in Senior Third and—"

"Who is the most handsome boy in your class?"

"There aren't any," I replied, feeling uneasy.

Helena twiddled the ribbons tied around her braids. "Well… Richard is good-looking if he combs his hair." I stared at her. Rotten, snowball-throwing Richard?

"Speaking of hair," said Senja, pulling the front sections of her straw-coloured tresses forward, "I want bangs. A girl on the train had gorgeous black hair with bangs." Helena hung on her every word. "My mother says no, but perhaps I will cut them myself."

Helena said, "You will?"

I arched my eyebrows. "I think that's dumb."

"Saara, dear, when you become a young lady, you will be more concerned with your appearance. Won't she, Helena?"

The unsettled feeling congealed into a bitter lump in my stomach. I wished that Mama had never agreed to our pastor's request. But a promise was a promise. Taking a deep breath, I said, "When you go to school, the teacher will ask your name, so let's practise English."

"I suppose I should," she said, rolling her eyes.

"Say, 'My name is Senja Kallio.'"

"My… name… is… Senja Kallio."

"Well done," said Helena. "To say your age is, 'I am thirteen.'"

48

"I… am… tir… tirteen." As she struggled with the "th" I considered correcting her, but remembered how long it had taken Helena to pronounce English words properly.

"You should explain where you are from," I added. "Say, 'I came on a ship from Finland.'"

"I came… on sip—"

Without thinking I corrected, "I came on *a ship*—"

Helena switched to English to say, "Saara, don't be so fussy. That's too long a sentence for a beginner."

"I'm sorry, Senja," I said.

Pastor Hannunen cleared his throat. "It is time for us to leave." The sky was darkening.

"Goodbye, Senja," said Helena. "See you tomorrow at *my* house."

Outside, the north wind whooshed down my coat's open collar. I knotted my scarf tightly around my neck. I couldn't wait to have the new girl settled and get back to just Helena and me.

The principal decided against placing Senja in Senior Fourth with students her age, or even in Junior Fourth, but instead assigned her to our class. Mr. McKee sat her next to Helena. They were allowed to whisper so that Helena could translate the lessons.

It was difficult to concentrate on arithmetic as it was, with Papa's bad mood clouding mine. But with Helena and Senja sitting three rows ahead, shoulders jiggling, the long division problem on my desk made no sense. I wondered what could possibly be humorous about it.

When Senja pointed at me I knew their laughter had nothing to do with school work. The spark of jealousy in my heart burst into flame.

Knocking my scribbler to the floor "by accident" had the desired effect. Mr. McKee looked up and noticed the girls' behaviour. "Helena, your enthusiasm is commendable," said Mr. McKee, "however, you are disturbing others. Quiet, now."

That was all? No punishment? How disappointing.

After a weekend spent helping Mama with spring cleaning—beating the dirt out of every mat and scrubbing every floor—I ran to catch up to Helena and Senja on their way to school on Monday. Panting, I said, "Did you see… the cleanup notice… in the *Daily News*?" My excitement eased the hurt of their not waiting for me so that we could walk together.

Senja planted her hands on her hips and screwed her face as if she smelled something foul. "*We* do not bother with the local paper."

"I've been translating 'Home Loving Hearts' from the *Free Press* for Senja," said Helena.

I ignored their comments and continued. "It's an easy way to earn money—a dime a barrel for rubbish gathered from vacant lots."

"You can use the money for your trip!" said Helena. Senja glared at me.

"Let's start right after school," I said. "We can—"

"Come, Helena," said Senja, tilting her nose to the sky. "We are going to be late."

At dismissal, Helena approached my desk, staring at her wringing hands. "I... I can't do the cleanup. I... forgot that Mama needs me to help bake pies. Good luck."

"Helena, wait." But she sped toward the doorway where Senja stood, arms crossed, lips curled in a smirk.

"*I* think it's a fine project," I mumbled. How odd that Mrs. Pekkonen would bake pies on washday.

It took two days of stooping to pick up rusty tins and soggy papers during my spare time to fill one barrel. I should have waited until more snow had melted, as it made finding the rubbish difficult. I wondered if it was worth it. Handing my hard-earned dime to Mama, I said, "You can put this toward our tickets."

"Bless you." She added the coin to the coffee-tin bank in the rear of the cupboard.

After Mr. McKee dismissed us on Thursday, I found Helena waiting outside the classroom, alone.

"Where's Senja?"

"At a doctor's appointment. Do you want to come over?"

"Okay." I grinned as if I'd won first prize.

"Didn't Richard look dashing in his new shirt when he did his Silver Islet presentation?"

"He's the same old Richard to me."

"Senja thinks he's handsome."

I frowned and stomped on a clump of snow. An uncomfortable silence hedged between us for the rest of the way.

"Hello, girls," said Mrs. Pekkonen, stirring the huge

soup pot. "Saara Mäki, you're as thin as a rake. Have a piece of *näkkileipä* with butter and cheese."

Helena fetched two bottles of Coca-Cola from the porch and asked, "May we please have these?"

Mrs. Pekkonen said, "You may share one. You know they cost a whole nickel each."

"Thank you." Helena opened one brown bottle and divided it between two glasses. Mama didn't let me have the soft drink or chew Coca-Cola gum, either. I would have as much as I wanted when I grew up.

In Helena's room, we sat on her bed, crunching the dark rye dried bread. The butter tasted extra delicious since Mama had begun to ration ours to Sundays. Before I could tell Helena about my money-making efforts, she shook her head, whipping her braids around her, and said, "I can't believe it."

"What?"

"Senja's mother is allowing her to have bangs. Did you know she sneaks her mother's rouge and tries it on her cheeks?"

I stopped sipping my drink and made a face. Helena asked, "What?"

"Senja this, Senja that—you'd think she's royalty the way you dote on her. You never used to fuss about your hair or think the boys are handsome. It makes me want to retch."

Helena gave me a knowing smile. "You will change your mind when you get older."

Never.

5

It was Easter Sunday. Auntie and Uncle were coming in time for supper—if there was enough snow for their sleigh to pass. At church, Papa sat tall, arms folded across his chest, staring at Pastor Hannunen preaching the sermon. In the row ahead, Mr. Lahti's head drooped, then snapped up. He yawned, rubbing his eyes. My legs still felt the sting of Papa's switch from the day before. All over silly raisins! I'd helped myself to some of the ones Mama had saved for Easter. I wriggled on the hard pew, trying to concentrate as the pastor droned on. I imagined God, grey-bearded on His throne in Heaven, shaking His finger at me, saying, "Thou shalt not steal raisins."

That afternoon, I was the first to spot Uncle's sleigh. I ran out ahead of everyone else to hug Aunt Marja and exclaimed, "You've certainly grown!"

She chuckled. "Can you believe the birth is still two months away? You've grown even taller and more lovely since New Year's."

A glow spread through me. With my aunt I could do nothing wrong. With my father I could do nothing right.

Uncle Arvo lightly tugged one of my braids. "Have you got your steamship tickets?"

"No, not yet." I frowned. "Saving money is so hard! I was earning a little cleaning up vacant lots, but when Papa found out he forbade me to continue." I made my voice low and stern. *"No child of mine is a trash collector."*

"Don't give up, Saara. Somehow your prediction will come true."

Shrugging, I gave him a weak smile as the rest of my family spilled out of the house to greet them.

Auntie embraced Mama, then John, though he tried to avoid her reach.

"Hello," said Uncle Arvo, shaking Papa's hand. "How are the job prospects?"

"There is talk of work at the docks as soon as the ice clears and ships can navigate the bay again."

"Good luck there." Uncle signalled for me to help him unhitch his horse. Papa hoisted a basket of potatoes out of the sleigh and ushered the others indoors.

For supper Mama served pork roast—tinier portions than usual—and lots of gravy and vegetables. I missed her fancy desserts. We made do with un-iced pound cake and fruit soup.

Papa sipped his coffee, then said, "Of the few small jobs I've had so far, the best was three days on a Finnish construction crew. The pay was *twenty* cents per hour."

"I know you want steady work," said Auntie, "but for

now I hope you find more of those types of jobs." She smiled at Mama.

"Without me working full-time, I didn't think we could manage to keep saving for a house, but we are."

Auntie and Mama exchanged worried looks. They were probably thinking what I was thinking. *What about the trip to Finland?*

Monday was a holiday from school, so I'd been reading since Auntie and Uncle left after lunch. Yawning, I closed *Anne of Avonlea*, placed the library book on my bed, and stretched like Sipu. I guessed it was time to set the supper table, so I headed to the stairs.

Papa's voice thundered below. "All my growing-up years on the farm we struggled to keep the family in shoes." A lid on the wood stove clanked into its round hole.

Mama said, "Marja and Arvo have—"

"Have what? A comfortable life? No. A secure income? No."

"They are happy and have enough."

I sat on the top step to wait out their "discussion." Sipu curled herself around my arm and climbed onto my lap, purring.

"Once I have full-time work I'll be happy too," said Papa. "Then we can buy a house—"

"Happy? No. You will never have enough." Mama spoke much louder than she usually did. "Loving each other and appreciating our heritage are far more important than all our possessions."

I stared at the farm scene woven into the woollen tapestry hanging on the wall. There were flowers, big trees, and a grain shed. In front of the farmhouse stood a girl feeding chickens. Near the bottom, next to a horse and a goat, was a couple holding hands. The images appealed to me: loving parents, animals, and no brother. If only...

All I could hear were regular cooking noises: the icebox door closing, a stick of wood being shoved into the stove, and Mama singing a hymn. It was safe to enter the kitchen.

It was easy to steer clear of Papa over the next two weeks. Mama had me deliver a record number of completed garments to her customers and collect payments.

Heading home from school on Friday with Helena and "Her Majesty, Queen Senja," I asked, "Are you going to the play tonight?"

"Of course we are," said Helena. "Are you?"

"Yes."

"That's terrific."

Senja gave me a sugary smile. "I'm surprised, with your family so poor, the money is used for anything besides laundry soap or the rent."

I bristled. How a person could sound so sweet, yet be so cruel, was beyond me. It was true that we had missed all of the other plays since February. If it weren't for Papa volunteering to organize the library and being given free tickets, we would not be going tonight. But we weren't as badly off as Senja seemed to think.

"My mother's had so much extra sewing work, we'll have enough for steamship tickets soon," I boasted.

"Do you *still* think you will go to Finland?" asked Helena. "I'll believe it when I see your ticket."

Something shifted painfully deep inside me. She doubted what I'd said.

Senja smirked. "You know why your father has no regular job, don't you? No one wants to hire a strike organizer. They're troublemakers."

"That's not true!" Or was it? Shame cramped my insides. If only Papa hadn't gone on strike, he'd still have his job and we'd have our passage to Finland booked.

Senja veered into Barton and Fisher's hardware store, pulling Helena along with her. "I need a bottle of paste."

Good riddance! I was so cross I didn't even stop to pat Blackie, the dark horse hitched to the Kivelä Bakery wagon. I marched straight home.

After supper, Mama rouged and powdered her cheeks. Papa looked handsome dressed in his best suit. When we arrived at the Big Finn Hall auditorium for the Finnish Drama Society's play, I sat with my parents and John. I glanced over my shoulder. The curved balcony brimmed with families. Drat. Helena and Senja were sitting behind us.

Act One began. Every time an actor delivered a funny line, Papa roared. I'd forgotten how heartily he could laugh. When I joined in, the seams of my dress felt as if they might burst. I was putting off asking Mama to sew a new Sunday dress for me, but I couldn't make do with the green one much longer.

During the finale, the actress playing Fiina batted her eyelashes and swooned into the character Erik's arms. Senja aahed and Helena sighed loudly. I rolled my eyes. When Fiina recovered, she and Erik swore to love each other forever. The look she gave Erik convinced me. In my parents' wedding portrait, Mama's face held the same expression. No smile, of course, but eyes full of love. Yet, from the way Mama and Papa argued, it seemed their love hadn't lasted forever.

Later, Mama stuck her head into my bedroom and asked, "Did you say your prayers?"

"Yes. I asked God why Papa isn't a farmer like Uncle Arvo."

Mama chuckled and perched on my bed. "God is the only one who could convince him, he is so set in his ways."

"Like how he always scolds me."

"Not always—"

"Yes, always. No matter how hard I try, he finds a fault. Yesterday my potato peels were too thick. Today Sipu's water dish was too far from the wall. Even when I earned money he exploded."

Mama sighed and stretched her shoulders back. "There is a great deal on his mind. He's focused on providing for us."

I mumbled, "Then he should never have gone on strike."

"Saara, you will not speak against your father that way. Be proud that he stands up for what he believes is right."

She smoothed my hair away from my face. "He may not show his love in the way you want him to, but it doesn't mean he doesn't love you."

I stroked Sipu's curved back. "Do you love Papa?"

"Of course I do."

"At times you sound so angry."

"We have disagreements, but I still love him." She paused. "He and I want different things." Her eyes held a faraway look, as if I were no longer there. "I pray he will find peace in his heart."

CHAPTER

6

Tubas, trumpets, and a big drum burst into sound. It was ten o'clock and the May Day parade had begun! Mr. Pekkonen, Helena, John, Fred, and I stood on the top step outside the Labour Temple to watch. Hurrah—no Senja! She had been asked to participate in the parade. The single cloud over the morning was having to mind my brother and his friend. The flag-bearers stepped out, the first one proudly carrying a huge red flag for socialism, the others, Union Jacks. Several rows of Fort William Finnish Bandsmen marched behind, filling the sunshine with bright notes.

In the excitement I'd forgotten to eat the pastry Mrs. Pekkonen had shoved into my hand before we left her and Mandi at street level. I took a bite of the sweet flaky treat, my toes tapping out the band's rhythm.

"There's Mama!" shouted John, pointing to a group of women parading past. Mama held up one side of a "WOMEN SHOULD VOTE" banner. We called out to her and waved, but it was as impossible for her to hear us with the band playing as it was to spot us among the masses of spectators on either side of Bay Street. I licked my sticky fingers. Another suffrage banner attached to poles bobbed along, followed by one that had the word "CHILD."

"Can you read that banner, Helena?" I asked.

"Yes. 'CHILD LABOUR MUST BE... ABUSED.'"

"Abused? Are you sure?"

Mr. Pekkonen shook his head. "It says, 'CHILD LABOUR MUST BE *ABOLISHED*.'"

"That makes more sense," I said, stifling a giggle.

Helena nudged my arm and asked, "Isn't that your father?"

I nodded. "John, do you see Papa?"

Two dozen gymnasts in white uniforms marched in step. First came the women, who wore the bows of their waist sashes draped to the left. The men followed. There was Papa, dressed in his sleeveless top, waistband, and white pants. The band music stopped for a moment, so I shouted, "PAPA!" and jumped up and down, both arms high in the air. He looked right at me and waved.

Row after row of ordinary people marched by— hundreds! John and Fred lost interest and began play-fighting.

"Stop that, John," I said, but he paid no attention to me. Mr. Pekkonen pulled them apart, then offered Wrigley's Spearmint gum to the boys and to Helena and me. I unwrapped my stick and popped it into my mouth. The fresh taste tingled my tongue.

"Here comes Senja!" said Helena.

Senja wore a white blouse, red bodice, and striped skirt. She was among eight girls who filed past, each wearing a different traditional costume, with five in Finnish dress.

"You wouldn't believe the fuss she made this morning—a tantrum, really. At first she refused to participate, then later agreed."

"What did she get her mother to promise?" I said.

Helena laughed. "Trust Senja to get her way—with the promise of a store-bought dress and that she'd never have to wear the Finnish outfit again."

Hundreds more participants marched along, mostly Finlanders. The parade seemed endless! At last the final marchers appeared and many in the crowd followed them along their route down Bay Street. We climbed down the steps to where Mrs. Pekkonen was tucking Mandi in her carriage. She said, "If we go directly to Ray Park, we can watch the parade arrive there before the speeches begin."

The boys ran ahead while Helena and I took turns pushing the carriage. Ray Park filled quickly with men, women, and children. A gentleman from Winnipeg gave the first address. I played with Mandi to pass the time.

After the final speech, my parents found us. "My arms are about to fall off," said Mama, groaning.

"That's what happens when you step out as a 'New Woman,'" said Papa, winking at John and me. "Next they'll be saying I'm married to Emilia *McClung*."

"Such a compliment. If anyone can get women the vote here in Canada, Nellie McClung can."

"Enough, enough."

"Papa, are you entering the half-mile foot race?" I

asked. "Or the discus throwing?"

"I cannot think about the sports program until we complete our gymnastics demonstration." He glanced over his shoulder. "They're taking their positions without me!"

Papa dashed over to join the line of gymnasts. He dropped onto his hands and knees on the ground. A woman stepped up on his back, grasping the hand of another woman who balanced on the outstretched linked arms of two men. Altogether the group built a human pyramid four people tall at the highest point. I cheered and clapped along with the crowd.

When the demonstration was over, Papa walked toward us rubbing his lower back. "I strained a muscle doing the pyramid. No sports for me this afternoon."

"I want to be in a pyramid someday," said John. Papa patted him on the shoulder.

Following our late lunch at home, Mama sank onto a kitchen chair. "I need to rest for a while. Pass me the mending basket, will you, Saara? Tauno, you should lie down and relax your back. I will make coffee in an hour or so."

Papa winced as he stood and headed upstairs. John left to play with Fred. I was wound up from the festivities and couldn't decide what to do.

"Saara, could you read the newspaper to me?" said Mama, mending the heel of a sock. "I should try to learn this English."

I picked up the *Port Arthur Daily News*, scanned the

front page, and read aloud, "*The first-place winner in the public school contest for keeping the neatest work books was Toini Jarvela.*"

"Mrs. Jarvela will be sure to clip that notice," said Mama, "and show it to everyone after church on Sunday."

"*The new captain of the Canadian Pacific steamship Empress* of Ireland *is Henry George Kendall.*"

"They say the *Empress of Ireland* is Canada's most luxurious steamer. If we can somehow get the remaining money, we should have enough for third-class passage on the *Empress.*"

That reminded me to read the classified section to find work I could do. For a laugh, I always read the ads carefully, searching for poor grammar. Last week there was *Wanted—A man to take care of horses who can speak German.* Another time I'd found *Wanted—A furnished room by a lady about 16 feet square.*

After a minute of silent reading, I giggled and read aloud, "*For sale—A nice large dog, will eat anything, very fond of children.*" Mama looked confused. I began to explain the humour to her in Finnish, but then another ad caught my eye. *LOST—Grey mare, weighs about 1200 pounds. Reward to finder. Phone North 916 or call 424 Dawson Street.*

A reward! "Where would a hungry horse go?"

"What?"

"There's a missing horse. May I go and have a look around?"

"Fine, but—"

64

"I know, be home for supper."

A coiled rope in the porch caught my eye. Slipping it over my shoulder, I muttered, "Where would the mare go to look for food?"

Outside, John and Fred were playing marbles. I considered the spilled grain by the grain elevator. To get there, the mare would have to cross a main street and two sets of railway tracks. "No, horses are too skittish," I mumbled.

"Johnny, does your sister always talk to herself like that?" asked Fred. They snickered.

Without a single glance at the boys, I turned and ran down the back lane, heading to the Star Livery. Elias was the person to ask for some ideas. I found him brushing a bay horse with swift strokes.

"Miss Saara! Come to see Chief again, have you?"

"No, I'm searching for a lost grey mare."

"Ain't seen one around here."

"Do you think she'd go to the cow pasture north of the city?"

He rested his elbow on the bay's rump, pointing his brush at me. "Nah, the grass ain't grown yet. She'd be lookin' for hay's my guess."

I checked the City Stables and the Northern Livery but nobody had seen a mare on the loose. One groom said she'd likely keep to the outskirts of town, that I'd find her on a farm somewhere.

I pondered and puzzled as I marched up the Bay Street hill, past my lookout spot and the newly completed mansions on Summit Avenue. Golly, one of those houses was big enough for at least four families.

Two blocks farther, I crossed the streetcar tracks. At the city's western limit, the Hodges' farmhouse and barn came into view. So did their vicious dogs. I flinched. The mare would definitely shy away from those creatures.

I visited the neighbouring property to the north, and even had a look in their barn, but found no grey mare. My feet began to ache. The rope I carried made my neck itch. The hunt was futile. I figured I should give up and go home.

On the other side of a stand of pussy willows, I saw Mrs. Niemi's farm. Her husband had passed away the previous summer. She still lived on the property but had sold the livestock. Could the mare have found her way into the barn to eat the leftover hay? I trotted to the dirt driveway and turned in.

Mrs. Niemi opened the door as I reached the steps. "Good afternoon, Saara," she said in Finnish. She wore a long black dress, an apron, and a close-fitting white hat.

"Good afternoon, Mrs. Niemi. I'm looking for a grey horse. Have you seen one?"

"No. I have not been well the past few days. You are welcome to have a look around."

"Thank you. I'll try the barn first. Goodbye."

"Say hello to your mother for me. God bless you."

I slid the rope off my shoulder and unwound one end. How hard would it be to catch the horse if she was there? What if she wore no halter? Would she spook and rear or kick? My heart beat faster.

The barn door was ajar. I crept inside and smelled

fresh manure. A rustling came from the rear of the barn. Tingly warmth raced up my backbone. There stood a grey horse.

The mare saw me and startled. I jerked, heart pounding. She backed up, flung her head high, and snorted.

Moving quietly forward, knees shaking, I reminded myself to do what Uncle Arvo had taught me. *Keep your arms down. Act as though you have no intention of catching the horse.*

The mare wove from side to side, looking past me to the open door. I chided myself for not closing it earlier. Drawing nearer to her, I realized I wouldn't be able to catch her if she charged. The mare was enormous.

I had to get her head down. Slowly I returned the coiled rope to my shoulder and bent to pick up a bucket. Scooping a handful of dirt into the bucket, I shook it, hoping the pebbles sounded like grain.

The mare's ears twitched forward, her head lowered, and she stepped toward me. We were a few feet apart. As she bent her neck to sniff inside the bucket, I eased my fingers upward and took hold of her halter. I carefully set the bucket on the ground, then attached the rope securely to her halter.

"Good girl," I crooned. "I'm going to call you 'Lady.' You had quite a feast, Lady, didn't you?" As she calmed, I stroked her face and neck. Her eyes closed.

Hurrah! The reward would be mine.

I led the mare out to the driveway and began to run, but Lady refused to do more than plod. At her pace it could take an hour to get to her owner's house. A "V" of geese flew overhead, honking their way north, while a woodpecker hammered a roadside poplar.

How much would the reward be? Whatever the amount, it meant we would be closer to getting the tickets.

My feet and neck prickled with heat when we eventually reached Dawson Street. "Here's number 424, Lady."

I tied the mare to a birch tree out front and knocked on the door. When a heavy-set gentleman appeared, I said, "Hello, sir. Is this your grey mare?"

"Where did you... how...?" he sputtered. "You're a slip of a girl."

"She gorged on hay and likely has a stomach ache." I wanted to mention the reward but bit my lip to hold back the words.

"Apart from her swollen belly, she looks fine," the man said, smiling. "I promised a reward, but didn't expect to pay a child, let alone a girl. Wait here." He limped away, leaning on a cane.

Would he give me a quarter? Or maybe a fifty-cent piece?

Lady's owner returned and handed me an envelope. "What is your name?"

"Saara Mäki, sir."

"Saara, don't you spend all of this on sweets. Think of something special."

"Thank you, sir."

I ran several blocks before daring to peek inside the packet, realizing it contained no coins. Air rushed into my open mouth. My eyes bulged. There were five one-dollar bills. After a week of dirty, back-straining work I had filled two trash barrels, worth only twenty cents. Now I had earned fifty barrels' worth of cash for an afternoon of horse hunting. My feet barely met the ground as I raced home. Papa would be so proud of me. Mama would be thrilled.

Three blocks away, a gust of westerly wind flapped my dress above my knees. Dark clouds snuffed out the sunlight. Chilled, I ran on. At Dufferin Street, my leg muscles burned as if on fire, screaming to stop. When I slowed to a walk it dawned on me. There were no children outside playing. I was late for supper, but how late, I didn't know. Fat raindrops plopped on my head.

Opening the door of our house, I heard the clatter of dishes entering the sink. Mama was clearing the table. I had my answer: very late.

"Child, where have you been?" Mama's usually ruddy cheeks were pale.

"You had better have a good reason," added Papa.

"You're in big trouble," whispered John.

"Look at my reward!" I said, fanning out the bills like playing cards. "My hunch was right about Lady."

Papa looked puzzled. Mama's jaw hung down. John's eyes popped out of his head.

"What lady are you talking about?" asked Papa. "Reward for what?"

"Lady is what I call the grey horse that went missing from Dawson Street. I read about her in the newspaper. She was at Mrs. Niemi's farm."

"Are you claiming you captured a runaway horse and

returned it to Dawson Street where the owner gave you five dollars?"

"Yes," I said, confused.

John blurted in English, "Golly gee. Did you chase it and lasso it?"

I shook my head. "It can all go toward our trip."

"This is wonderful," said Mama.

Papa's fist crashed on the table. "Saara, stop dreaming of traipsing halfway around the world. There is no trip. Not unless Mama could earn a decent wage instead of sewing for nickels and dimes."

Mama sucked in a breath, started to respond, and exhaled. How could Papa say that? He knew how hard she worked, sewing and taking care of John when he was sick and cooking and cleaning. Besides, I knew her "nickels and dimes" were often fifty-cent pieces.

"My daughter brings home more money in one afternoon than I earned all week," grumbled Papa. I stared at my feet. He huffed out, banging the door. His anger stung and put a dint in my pride. I prayed he wouldn't notice the rope was gone. In my excitement I had left it behind.

CHAPTER

7

Lady and the reward money filled my thoughts. It was impossible to focus all day at school on Monday, until late in the afternoon when Mr. McKee described the upcoming Empire Day exercises.

"We will practise several songs for the assembly," he said, "plus one student from my class will be responsible for a recitation."

Most pupils in front of me stared at their desks, likely hoping they wouldn't be chosen, but I sat tall and smiled at Mr. McKee.

He scanned the rows. "I see a few eager faces." He looked at me. "I am assigning the recitation of 'The Children's Song' to you, Saara. You will need to stay after school and carefully copy the text into your scribbler."

"Yes, sir." *Thank you!*

I skipped all the way home. I could hardly wait to tell Papa. When I arrived, Mama was way behind on the washing. As she stirred the trousers and soapy water in the boiler with her stick, I realized she was weeping.

"Mama, what's wrong?"

She replaced the long oval lid on the boiler and pulled an envelope from her apron pocket. "A letter came from Aili today. Our mother is… is sick." She wiped tears from her face. "We must go home to Finland soon."

After Empire Day, I hoped. "Do we have enough money saved?"

"Not for all of us. There's almost enough for three." She pocketed the letter. "But time is running out. Even if Papa won't go, we must."

Would Mama travel all that way without Papa? It would take nearly two weeks to get to Finland and we'd be away for three months altogether.

When Papa came home, he smiled at me. "Another shipment of books arrived for the library. Is my helper available on Saturday?"

"Yes, Papa." I beamed. "She certainly is."

His worry lines were gone and he sounded almost carefree. "There are several stories you would enjoy reading."

"Papa, I was picked—"

"Supper is ready," said Mama, her voice shaky. We sat down to eat and before I could finish telling Papa what had happened at school, Mama told him Aili's bad news.

Papa sagged in his chair. "We cannot afford the passage to the Old Country."

My heart bounced against my ribs.

"Tauno, my mother is seriously ill." Mama wrung her apron with trembling fingers. "And she has never seen her grandchildren."

"We're scraping by on what I make with these odd jobs. We will never be able to buy our own house if we use up our savings."

Mama released her apron and stood tall. "Is that more important to you than family? I don't care about owning a house. The children and I need to see my mother before she dies."

Papa held his head in his hands. He rubbed his temples.

Would my exciting news cheer him? "Papa, I'm giving the most important recitation at school on Empire Day."

"That's my girl." He didn't look up.

After a moment I said, "In the newspaper it said the Port Arthur Laundry wants to hire girls. I could work there."

"By 'girls' they mean at least fourteen years old, not children," said Papa. I blushed.

"Could I be a newsboy?" said John.

"Jussi, work hard at school," said Papa. "Education will get you a good job. Saara wants to be grown up. Perhaps she will marry a rich man and we will never need to worry about money again."

Inside my head I shouted, *I want to do more in my life than marry a rich man*. I clenched my teeth. Forgetting about the spoon of blueberry soup in my hand, I let two purple drops splash on my dress.

"Saara, be more careful," said Mama. "You know how blueberries stain. Get the Sunlight soap and—"

"I know what to do. You don't have to tell me."

"Do not raise your voice to your mother," said Papa.

"Can't hold a spoon straight and she wants to work in a laundry. She'd get her fingers crushed in the wringer."

"I'm sorry, Mama." I ran upstairs to change. Returning with the soiled dress, I grasped the bar of yellow soap and scrubbed vigorously.

"Stop," said Mama, "or you'll wear a hole through your dress."

Now even Mama thought I couldn't do anything right!

That night in bed, I could hear my parents arguing downstairs. Green and mauve northern lights danced across the clear sky. I stared at my lead boat from New Year's Eve on the dresser, wishing once again that Uncle's prediction would happen for real.

All week Mama's sewing machine treadled more than ever. She increased my share of the household chores, so that she would have more time to sew. That left me with little time to read over "The Children's Song," let alone work on memorizing the verses.

On Friday morning Papa came downstairs scowling. "Emilia," he said, "who ironed my shirt, the cat? It's still wrinkled."

"Saara is giving me a hand with—"

"You mean the same girl who thought she could get a job at the Port Arthur Laundry?"

"Tauno, she's learning."

"Have her practise on her own clothes. I'll have to keep my jacket on all day and get overheated."

That night after supper I propped my scribbler open

above the sink so that I could work on my recitation as I washed the dishes. I thought I knew the first couple of lines, but they weren't sticking. I circled the last greasy plate with my soapy dishcloth and sighed.

"Why so glum?" Mama slipped her arm around me. "Come and count the trip savings with me."

I dried my hands, grabbed the tin, and dumped the contents on the table. We grouped the coins into one dollar piles and totalled the amount.

"We need only three or four dollars more, Saara! See how much closer we are to our goal?"

"But I thought Papa doesn't want us to go."

"He is upset, but the three of us will go—you, me, and Jussi. I would have us leave today if I could." Mama replaced the coins in the tin, then lifted her mending basket onto the table and began to repair the torn hem of my brown gingham dress.

After I drained and rinsed the sink, I swept the floor. The front door banged shut and John called, "Mr. Koski is here!"

Mama threw down her mending and whispered, "Has Marja had the baby early?" She rushed down the hallway with me close behind.

"Good evening, Mrs. Mäki," said Mr. Koski.

"How is Marja?"

"Fine. Still waiting for the baby to come." He withdrew a tied handkerchief from his jacket pocket. "She asked me to deliver this to you. For the trip to see your mother."

She had to have received a letter from Aili, too.

"Thank you. Will you stay for coffee?"

"No, thank you. I need to be on my way."

Mama saw him out, then untied the handkerchief. "Dear Marja," she said, grinning. "This must be all of her egg money."

I gaped at the coins and bills: four whole dollars. Mama hugged me, then John.

Staring at Mama, I said, "Does this mean—"

"Yes, Saara. We buy our tickets tomorrow!"

I shot out the door to Helena's. She answered my rapping, saying, "What's gotten into you?"

Out of breath, I said, "Aunt Marja… sent us money… for the trip. We have enough for the tickets! Pinch me so I know this is real."

She obliged, all too willingly.

I woke on the fringe of a dream, standing at the rail of a grand ship, watching the sunlight glitter on the water below. A gentle breeze tickled my skin. The image evaporated when I remembered it was the day to buy our tickets at the Canadian Pacific Railway station.

Wasting no time, I traded my nightgown for my undervest, fastened its garters to my stockings, then threw on my petticoat and dress. Tantalizing aromas wafted upstairs: Finnish pancakes, rhubarb soup, and boiled coffee. My stomach rumbled. I flew down the stairs.

Papa held a lump of hard sugar in his teeth and drank his coffee from the saucer. His stern face burst the joy-bubble inside me. I hardly dared to breathe as I sank into my chair. Mama's puffy, red eyes glistened as she served the thin pancakes. Would Papa forbid us to go?

Silence ruled the kitchen until my father stood to leave. Mama accompanied him to the front hall. I heard Papa's deep voice. Her reply was muffled.

Mama reappeared wearing her no-nonsense look. "Saara, get your hairbrush. Jussi, go ask Fred's mother to look after you for the morning." As she brushed the tangles out of my waist-length hair and rebraided it, she explained the details for purchasing our tickets. It would be my task to speak and translate for her.

"We must go before my courage deserts me." Mama emptied the coffee-tin bank into her leather handbag, except for two nickels each for streetcar fare.

Saturday shoppers were laden with dry goods from the Co-op, wrapped shirts from Sam Sing Laundry, packages of meat from the butcher, or rye bread, still warm from Kivelä Bakery's oven. Passing the Big Finn Hall, I scanned the wide stairs hoping Papa wouldn't be among the throng of fedora-crowned men smoking out front. There was no sign of him.

"Look at this!" John's cheerful voice startled me from behind. He and Fred held up shiny objects. "The Coca-Cola man gave me a pocket knife for keeps."

"I wish I'd been there," I said. "I wonder what Mr. Ruohonen gives to girls?"

"Jussi," said Mama, "what are you doing here?"

"Fred's mother had to go to the butcher."

"Go back there and wait for her."

Mama resumed walking. "I'm relieved we did not see

your father." Her knuckles were white from gripping her handbag. "He might have talked me out of this foolishness."

Neighs, stomping hooves, and a pungent odour announced the Star Livery. *Good morning, Chief.* I window-shopped as we passed the Home Candy Kitchen. Directly ahead, past the maze of overhead wires, towered the massive grain elevator by Lake Superior.

Our timing was perfect. A streetcar approached Bay Street. When it stopped, we grabbed the skinny black pole to pull ourselves up onto the wooden platform, dropped our nickels in the cash box, and found an empty seat. The streetcar trundled eastward until it rounded the corner at Cumberland. The main street teemed with horse-drawn wagons, several automobiles, and pedestrians crossing from one side to the other, at every point but the intersections.

Stepping off the streetcar near Arthur Street, we headed into the Royal Bank to withdraw the rest of the money for our fares. We walked downhill to Water Street and along it past the Pagoda—the Port Arthur Publicity Office—with its stone beaver above the doorway. Ahead stood the red brick clock tower of the CPR station.

While waiting in line at the ticket office I picked up a colour brochure. It showed the RMS *Empress of Ireland* proudly cutting through calm, green water. *"Less than four days at sea,"* it read. The ship was gigantic, making the river pilot's boat alongside the *Empress* look like a toy.

"May I help you?" asked the station agent behind the counter.

"Yes, sir. Three tickets to Finland, please."

"Tell him we want to leave as soon as possible," whispered Mama.

I explained her concern, gave our names, my age, and John's, and requested the second-class rate for the train.

"If you wish to pay less," he said, "Colonist class is available."

"Yes, please." Then I added, "Is it possible to go on the *Empress of Ireland*?"

"Ah, the 'Queen of the Atlantic.' Yes, her next sailing may be the first available passage for you. Would you prefer a second-class or third-class cabin, Miss? They give special attention to third-class passengers nowadays. Not like it used to be."

"Third class, please."

"One way or return?"

"Return, please, for late August."

He consulted the steamship sailing dates and the eastbound train timetable. The big wall clock seemed to take an hour to mark the passing of five minutes, making my thoughts run wild. How long would we have to wait until we could leave Port Arthur? Would we miss the wedding after all? I chewed on a braid.

"You are in luck. You can leave May 26, arrive in Montreal May 27, take the *Empress Special* train to the city of Quebec the next morning, and board the *Empress of Ireland* for a late afternoon departure to Liverpool."

Liverpool was in England. How would we get the rest of the way to Finland?

"The rates include board, of course," he continued,

"and transfer of baggage across England and on a North Sea steamer to Hango, Finland."

When he calculated Mama's fare I gulped. We didn't have three times that amount.

"Since you and your brother are both under twelve you are charged half-fare."

Mama had to have known that because her figuring was exactly right. Relieved, I interpreted the details for her. She nodded and said, "Ask him where we could stay overnight in Montreal."

Before I could translate her question into English, the man said, "I could book an inexpensive room for you at the Queen's Hotel in Montreal. It's a short walk from Windsor Station."

Mama agreed when I explained.

"I must arrange the steamship passage by telegram, so you will need to come back tomorrow to pick up your tickets."

We returned the next afternoon. Mama carefully counted out the money while the station agent wrote our information on the tickets.

Outside of the train station, I felt like jumping, shouting, and laughing all at once. Our big official tickets lay folded and tucked inside Mama's handbag. Papa hadn't stopped us after all! Helena would have to believe that we were going. Uncle Arvo's New Year's prediction was coming true.

8

After the months of waiting and wondering, in less than two weeks we'd be on our way. Daydreaming about the trip became my favourite pastime. Thank goodness I still had ten days to perfect my recitation.

"Saara, I have something to ask you," said Mama. She covered the bread dough with a clean tea towel. "Let's sit down. The Sewing Circle ladies want to encourage new members to join, even younger ones your age. We have interesting talks about temperance and suffrage and—"

"Excuse me, Mama. What did you want to ask me?" My mind was on "The Children's Song."

"I want you to invite Helena and Senja."

Scowling, I said, "Senja never likes my ideas. And if she thinks something is stupid, Helena does too." I got louder with each sentence. "All they talk about is having a beau and how to fix their hair."

Mama's eyebrows knit together. "That explains why you spend more time reading than you do with them." She pushed back her chair and opened her arms wide. In her embrace I released the flood of tears I'd been holding back for weeks. Mama stroked my head. "Perhaps you need to make a new friend—a girl who shares more of your interests."

Mama must have felt sorry for me because she excused me from my chores. I wanted to forget about my problems by studying the poem or escaping into a book, but her suggestion hounded me. *Make a new friend.* It was impossible to imagine a best friend other than Helena. I was determined not to lose her. Out of habit, my legs marched me down to her house.

"Hello, stranger," said Mrs. Pekkonen.

Helena sat at the table using pincers to break up a large chunk of hard sugar.

"Do you want to play?" I asked, with my fingers crossed.

"Mama, is this my last chore?"

"Yes. I'll call you when the tables need setting."

Helena brushed the sugar dust into her palm, popped it into her mouth, and mumbled, "What would you like to do?"

It took me until we were out on the back steps to say, "It's been ages since we played store. Do you still have the pretend money we made?"

Helena screwed up her face. "That's a child's game."

"I thought it would be fun. You used to enjoy it."

"Senja says make-believe is for babies."

Resentment stewed and bubbled inside me. "I wish I could send her on the next boat to the Orient."

"What? How can you say that about our friend?"

"You mean *your* friend. I'm too plain and childish to be Senja's friend."

"Don't be silly. Come on, let's play a card game."

"No, you don't want to play. I'm going home."

"Saara, that's not true. Come back."

Mama was right. I needed a new friend. I began serious make-believe, pretending Helena and Senja did not exist.

The supper table held three bowls of beef stew. Papa would not be home between his four-hour piece-work job and the labour meeting. I frowned, stifling a groan over the few shreds of gristly meat in the thin broth with potatoes, turnips, and onions. At least it wasn't rice pudding. Having pudding alone for supper was exciting the first few times. But it had been served twice in the past week, and now I craved meat.

Mama spoke of our upcoming trip. "At Juhannus there will be music and dancing and floating bonfires on the lake." She rolled her shoulders back. With her face glowing, she looked like a child waiting for Christmas. "It will be light outside until after midnight."

"Why so late?" asked John, fanning his stew.

"We will be farther north than here."

"What about the wedding, Mama?" I asked.

"Aili will be married outdoors near the stand of white birches." She clasped her hands under her chin, interlocking her fingers. She closed her eyes, and inhaled. "I can already smell the lilacs by the fence in my parents' yard."

I could, too. My favourite flower.

John shrugged. "It sounds a lot like Port Arthur, if you ask me."

"Except for the midnight sun and being around all the family," I pointed out. "May I have more stew?"

"Me, too?" asked John.

"Saara, serve one ladle each," said Mama, "then put the pot on the back of the stove for Papa. He will find a steady job soon and we shall eat like kings."

That night, kneeling beside my bed, I prayed *again* for a job for Papa.

Over breakfast there was another "discussion" about money. With no warning, Mama said, "Tauno, I could try to get a refund for our tickets."

I clenched my jaw so I wouldn't say, "Mama, don't. I'd rather live without meat altogether than not go."

An invisible iron passed over Papa's forehead, smoothing the creases. "No, Emilia. You and the children must go."

His words so surprised me that I came close to knocking over my full glass of milk.

He wasn't done. "I don't know how we will manage, but your mother needs you." Yet on his way out, he spun around. "Saara, how many times must I tell you?" he barked. "Make sure the woodbox is full before you go to bed."

"But—"

"There are only two sticks left."

"It's John's turn to do it."

"Since when did Jussi start doing kitchen work?" yelled Papa.

"Ever since Saara began running more errands for me," said Mama.

Again, I was surprised. Papa glared at John cowering in his chair. "Jussi, there is no playing after school until this woodbox is full. Heaping full." He stomped out. I'd never heard him speak so harshly to my brother.

There were only two days left to memorize "The Children's Song." On the way to school I carried my scribbler open to where I'd copied it out. After reading it over, I held my scribbler behind my back and said under my breath, *"Land of our Birth, we pledge to thee, Our toil and love in—"* No, that wasn't right. Ooh, why did those wagon wheels have to creak and crunch the stones so loudly? The noise made it hard to concentrate. *"Land of our Birth, we pledge to thee, Our love and toil in the years to be; When we are grown and take our place, As men and women—"* Ew! What was that horrible stench coming from the butcher's?

I tried again and made it through the second stanza. My brain was not behaving normally. Why couldn't I remember the lines better? Was it excitement about the trip? A twinge of panic fluttered in my stomach. I was determined to learn the entire poem before bedtime.

Mama had other plans for me. After supper she made me try on the new dress she was sewing for me in order to pin the hem. She chatted non-stop about the trip. I had no chance to review the lines in my head.

The next day I snatched every free moment to work on my recitation until I could rattle off all eight verses. Mr. McKee asked me to stay behind after dismissal.

"Are you ready for tomorrow, Saara?"

"Yes, sir."

He reached for a stack of four books on his desk. "Since you will miss the rest of the school year, I am lending these to you to keep up your reading skills."

I accepted the books with a wide grin. "Thank you, sir. I'll read them all." *Black Beauty* was one of my favourites. The other titles were new to me. I would save them for the trip.

On Friday afternoon, all pupils of South Ward Public School assembled in the kindergarten department. Sliding back the folding doors had turned the rooms into a large hall. After several patriotic songs, one of the teachers presented a talk on the flag. My mouth felt dry knowing I was to follow him.

"Saara Mäki will now recite Rudyard Kipling's 'The Children's Song,'" announced Mr. McKee.

I dared not meet anyone's eyes. Taking my position, I chose a spot to stare at on the back wall. I breathed deeply, and began. At the end of the first verse I hesitated. What came next? My mind was blank. Knees quivering, I swallowed and started over.

The words flowed. Fifth verse. *"Teach us to look in all our ends, On Thee for judge, and not our friends; That we... That we..."* Stumped! Shame ignited my face. Mr. McKee whispered something but I could make no sense of it. My stomach rolled. I bolted into the hallway and kept running, out of the school, up Cornwall Avenue, along Secord Street.

Blackie stood, patient as ever, hitched to a Kivelä Bakery wagon. My side ached so much I had to stop. I clutched the horse's neck and sobbed into his coat.

Blackie whinnied when his driver emerged from the bakery. I sneaked behind the wagon, keeping out of his sight. School would be over soon. Then I could go home. I prayed that Mama would be so focused on her last sewing job that she wouldn't talk to me.

From outside the front door I could hear the whir of her sewing machine through the open window. I crept up to my room.

Later I heard Mama bustling about the kitchen. I dreaded going downstairs, but it was time to help prepare supper. I pasted on a smile.

"There she is," said Papa, at the same time that John blew in from outdoors. Papa lowered his newspaper, laying it on the table. "Did you give a grand recitation?"

"Yes, Papa," I said, acting the part.

"More like a grand flop, if you ask me," said John.

"He wasn't asking you, was he?" I whispered, but the look I gave my brother intending to silence him only spurred him on.

"She got stuck and forgot the words!" John grinned. "Then she ran away from school."

"Forgetting lines happens to the best reciters," said Papa. "But being truant! And lying to me! How could you?" His voice was as cold and piercing as an icicle. I hung my head. "I'm ashamed of you. Bring me all of your books. You will do without."

I stood there, stunned. *Not my books!*

"Go."

Having few of my own made the task simple. I gathered them, plus the three from the public library and the four from Mr. McKee. Back in the kitchen, I arranged the books in two stacks on the table.

"These ones are homework." Surely he'd let me keep them.

"You are done with school, so you are done with homework, too."

Mama kept silent standing at the wood stove, her eyes fixed on the sizzling pan.

Bitterness and loathing ripped through me like fireworks. It was my turn to storm out of the house. I headed to Bay Street and up the hill to my lookout. Beyond a stand of low bushes lay the rocky outcropping with my "chair," a worn, perfect-fit slab.

I was spitting mad at Papa, at John, and at myself, too. Why had I lied? Papa would have found out soon enough even if John hadn't tattled. But to take my books away was cruel, especially to take the ones from Mr. McKee. "Papa's not fair!"

Gazing at the stringy clouds scudding eastward, I wished I didn't have to wait until Tuesday to escape from my father. The greyish-blue silhouette of the Sleeping Giant reminded me of the poem I'd memorized for the school Christmas concert:

> *When did you sink to your dreamless sleep*
> *Out there in your thunder bed?*
> *Where the tempests sweep,*

And the waters leap,
* And the storms rage overhead.*

"How do you stay so peaceful, when it rages around you?" With my insides churning, I wanted to know his secret. I decided to finish the poem aloud.

Were you lying there on your couch alone
* Ere Egypt and Rome were born?*
Ere the Age of Stone,
Or the world had known
* The Man with the Crown of Thorn.*

The winds screech down from the open west,
* And the thunders beat and break*
On the amethyst
Of your rugged breast,—
* But you never arise or wake.*

I travelled in my mind back to the concert, where I had stood before the audience, legs shaking, but my voice steady, clear, and haunting.

You have locked your past, and you keep the key
* In your heart 'neath the westing sun,*
Where the mighty sea
And its shores will be
* Storm-swept till the world is done.*

A wave of applause swept over me as I bowed. I

locked my eyes on Papa's broad smile. Since that night in December, he hadn't sung my song or told us any Finnish folk tales. Most often he wasn't home to say good night. I was convinced that he didn't love me anymore. Well, I'd succeeded at ignoring Helena so I decided, from that moment on, I would ignore my father, too.

On the way home I snapped birch twigs into bits and kicked stones out of my path. Once upstairs, I found that someone had closed my bedroom door. Sipu mewed from the other side. I opened the door, and as I bent to stroke her back, she purred.

Then I saw the puddle.

And where she'd shredded the corner of the rug with her claws.

"Sipu, you naughty cat!" My arm lashed out, hitting her. She howled and scuttled under the bed.

My pulse raced. Fuming, I lay on my stomach to look her in the eye. "How could you? You know better." She crouched in the darkest corner.

By the time I'd finished cleaning her mess and tucking the frayed bits of rug through to the back so Mama wouldn't notice them, I was calm.

"Here, Sipu." She wouldn't budge. "What's the matter?"

She hissed when I reached under the bed, then tore out of my room and down the stairs. The image of my hand striking her flashed before me. I sank to the floor. How could I have done that to her?

9

The Pekkonens treated my family, including Auntie and Uncle, to a farewell supper at the Co-operative Restaurant in the basement of the Big Finn Hall. Helena greeted me with an icy hello and thrust a slim package wrapped in plain paper at me.

"May I open it now?"

She shrugged. I untied the string and folded back the paper to reveal a brown leather-bound book filled with blank pages.

"I thought..." said Helena. "Mama thought you could use a journal."

"It's perfect. Thank you." Opening the journal's front cover, I hoped with all my heart to find a message like, *To my best friend in the whole world, Saara. Have a wonderful trip. I'll miss you so much. Love, your friend forever, Helena.* Instead, scrawled in pencil and barely legible, were five words: *To Saara, Best Wishes, Helena.* At least she had written something.

I bit into a peppery meatball and thought about how

being together, the two of us, with no Senja to boss us, reminded me of life before the other girl arrived. Helena and I were so happy then. I wished I hadn't chosen to ignore her.

"Helena," I began, my hands clammy, "Mama bought me new boots and she sewed a dress for me for the trip." Helena focused on her potatoes. "It's a lovely shade of blue…" I gave up because she had turned away to listen to the men. If they were so interesting, then I would listen, too, but pretend not to, since Papa was speaking.

"Surely I'll have a regular job before Emilia returns. It's time for my luck to turn."

Uncle Arvo put down his fork. "Tauno, I hope that is true. But remember, farmland costs only a dollar fifty an acre. I'll help you get started—"

"Why farm? There is more to life than fighting weeds and weather."

Mr. Pekkonen sipped his buttermilk, cleared his throat, and said, "My arm still is not right." He winced as he tried to lift the arm that had been injured at the logging camp. "I need someone to do maintenance two days a week. Tauno, if you are interested, we could make a trade—your labour for a meal every night."

Papa's face turned red. "I don't want your charity or your pity."

"I don't intend either," said Helena's father, keeping his voice even. "You would definitely earn your food."

Mrs. Pekkonen smiled. "We have a lot of work piled up. You would be doing us a favour."

Helena's *parents* knew how to be polite. I snuck a peek

at Helena. Her face was stony.

"Tauno," said Mama, "I'd feel better knowing you were eating more than cold bread and kippers while I'm gone."

The harsh lines around Papa's eyes softened. In a husky voice, he said, "Thank you. If I'm lucky enough to get a steady job I won't need to—"

"*When* the good Lord provides you with a steady job," said Mama, "I'm sure you can still eat with the Pekkonens and pay the going rate." Helena's parents nodded.

Papa shook his head. "Emilia, you are one stubborn woman—in your arguing..." Quietly he added, "...and your faith."

Once my plate was empty I asked to hold Mandi. Her chubby face overflowed her white bonnet. She grasped my finger and sucked on the end. That tickled.

Uncle Arvo had us in stitches telling us about their ornery cow refusing to be milked by anyone but Aunt Marja. Being a month away from having her baby, she had trouble bending over, let alone milking. "Maybe I ought to wear a dress and Marja's hat so that cow will stop kicking me."

Mandi jiggled in my arms as I laughed.

"Be careful with my sister," warned Helena, glowering at me.

The waitress cleared the supper dishes and offered dessert. John nodded, while Helena and I said, "Yes, please" in exact unison. I flashed a grin at Helena, and then reminded myself that I was supposed to be ignoring her.

"Oh, Emilia," said Aunt Marja, "I don't want to forget to give this to you." She handed a small, rectangular brown leather case to Mama. "It's a wedding gift for Aili."

Mama opened the case and held up Marja's silver sugar spoon. "But this was Mother's gift—"

"—when my first husband and I left for Canada." Her eyes welled with tears.

The waitress returned with ginger cookies and a tray of bowls filled with raisin-studded rice pudding. She placed a serving in front of each person and scurried away. John picked up his cookie, but Mama motioned to wait.

Aunt Marja continued, "After the *Titanic* struck an iceberg I climbed into a lifeboat without him. He was not allowed to board." We listened intently, even John. "'A later boat for me,' he shouted. Those were the last words I heard from him."

John turned pale and whispered, "Papa, what if our boat hits an iceberg?"

"There won't be any this late in the spring," said Papa.

"Besides," said Mr. Pekkonen in a hushed voice, "the *Empress of Ireland* has been crossing the Atlantic safely for years."

Auntie dabbed her eyes with a handkerchief. "I believed happiness would never find me again, but then I met Arvo." Uncle placed his hand over hers. She gave him the loving-forever look. Papa coughed. Mama's eyes glistened. Mandi started to fuss, so I passed her to Mrs. Pekkonen.

"Here I am, blubbering away when you have an exciting adventure ahead," said Aunt Marja. "So, either I send the spoon for Aili, or I send turnips. Which would you rather carry?" Everybody laughed.

"Can we eat dessert now?" asked John.

Mama granted permission and said, "I'm honoured to deliver your gift, Marja. I'll keep it safe." She tucked the spoon back into its case and slipped it in her handbag.

Mrs. Pekkonen leaned close to Mama and said, "Are you concerned about travelling with the possibility of war?"

"It's a minor squabble over there in Europe," said Mr. Pekkonen. "Nothing to worry about."

John wanted Helena and me to count our raisins to see who had the most. He gobbled his pudding and announced, "Twelve."

I focused on my pudding, counting the plump raisins as I ate. Helena detested raisins so she piled hers on the side and said, "I have fifteen."

Swallowing my last mouthful, I smirked. "Sixteen. I won."

"That figures," muttered Helena, sneering. "Saara always has to come first."

"That's not true."

"How do we know you didn't cheat?" She turned her back to me, folding her arms across her chest. I didn't only turn away from her; I shifted my chair, too.

CHAPTER

10

Our trip was about to begin. I couldn't keep still. A cool breeze off the lake ruffled the hem of my dress and blew a page of newsprint across the width of the CPR station platform. In order to see the clock in the station tower, I wandered close to the railway tracks. Quarter to nine. My heartbeat quickened—I'd be late for school. I chuckled at myself. There was no more school for me until September. Hurrah!

"Saara, come away from the tracks," called Mama, adjusting the pin of her new straw hat. The brim and crown were trimmed in blue silk velvet—not the plain style of hat she would buy for herself. The Women's Committee had presented it to her for the work she had done reviving the Sewing Circle. Rooting through her handbag, she said, "Where are the tickets?"

"Emilia, calm down," said Papa. "They are here in my hand."

"What about Auntie's wedding gift?" I asked.

"The spoon is in my handbag." Mama smoothed her

jacket over her skirt.

Leather suitcases, wood and metal trunks, carpet bags, and bundles tied with rope were piled along the platform. The first-class passengers congregated at the far end, where the rear of the train would stop.

"Jussi, get down," shouted Papa. John scuttled off the baggage wagon. "You must behave yourself and be a help to Mama. Promise me you will be good."

"Yes, Papa."

"Saara, I expect you to watch out for your brother."

John could watch out for himself. I didn't want to do anything for someone who had deprived me of reading.

"Saara, did you hear me?"

I nodded.

After a moment Papa said, "You have done such a fine job helping me organize the library, that when you get back you can help sign out books."

I said nothing to him, of course. By then, would he allow me to have books again?

In the midst of the bustle, excited chatter, neighing of horses, and honking of motor cars, a low rumble like thunder came from the south. I strained my ears. Was I hearing wheels on the tracks? An unmistakable train whistle announced the approaching eastbound daily.

I saw the locomotive's steam cloud first. The gigantic engine puffed and clanged, spewing smoke and cinders from its smokestack. I felt dwarfed. Suddenly Mama's hand clawed my arm, drawing me farther back from the rails. Wheezing and hissing, the train stopped with its baggage car in front of us. Steam gushed around our feet.

Two cars away, a trainman in navy blue jacket, trousers, and CPR cap swung to the ground and set down a portable step. Papa ushered us toward the man and showed him our tickets.

"The Colonist car is directly behind you."

"Thank you," said Papa, handing the tickets to Mama. He carried our two suitcases and bags inside the coach. He reappeared and said, "It's exactly like the one we rode in when we first came to Canada. Same hard benches. Did you pack blankets?"

"One. Our coats will work, as well. It's only overnight."

"Thirty-some hours on those seats gets mighty uncomfortable."

"Can't you come, too?" John asked, pouting and clinging to Papa's arm. "I'm afraid of going on that big boat."

"Hush now, Jussi," Papa said, pushing him away. "You must be brave."

While Mama reminded John of the cousins he'd soon be playing with in Finland, Papa faced me.

"Farewell, Saara." I stiffened and looked down in silence. Turning, I felt his hand brush the back of my head before I dashed up the steps into the train car. "Wait," called Papa, but I kept going. Finding a middle seat on the far side, I glued my eyes on the view through the sooty window, and willed myself to forget my father.

A woman and her young son claimed a section at the front. The Colonist car had sixteen pairs of slatted wooden seats that faced each other. Half were occupied by men, with a few ladies. There was a pot-bellied stove at the back, and from the high ceiling hung large round lamps.

A tall bearded man stood next to the seat behind me and pulled down a wooden hinged platform suspended by chains. "We'll use the upper berth to store our bags," he said to his companion. "More room for my legs that way." On either side of the train car, above the upper berths, was a row of tiny windows.

"All aboard!" shouted the conductor, accompanied by the ringing of the train bell. Mama and John clambered onto the train and sat opposite me; their eyes watery. My brother's jaws pumped. He was sucking a candy, I supposed.

Mama set down a cloth bag on the seat beside me. "You ran onto the train so fast Papa didn't have a chance to give this to you."

The train creaked and jolted forward. Opening the bag, I gaped. The books from Mr. McKee! We were rolling out of the station. I scrambled across the aisle to a vacant seat and looked out the window. There was Papa, waving. His expression said, "I'll miss you." I felt all mixed up. Too soon he disappeared from view. I hadn't even said goodbye.

With my familiar surroundings dropping out of sight, I tried to let go of my troubles and concentrate on the adventure ahead. Current River flowed beneath us as we crossed the bridge. The train gathered momentum leaving Port Arthur. As I returned to my seat I whispered farewell to the Sleeping Giant on my right, and to Auntie and Uncle to the west.

"Tickets, please," said a man with a cheerful moustached face. His navy blue CPR cap had the word

"CONDUCTOR" framed by gold stripes. While he inspected our tickets, I stared at his brass buttons. Each bore the image of a beaver surrounded by "CANADIAN PACIFIC."

"Going to visit the Old Country, are we?" he said, hooking an index finger in his stiff white collar to loosen his bow tie. "It will be a warm one today." He returned our tickets and proceeded to the next section of high-backed seats.

The small boy at the front moved into the aisle and shouted, "Hello, Mister." His mother wagged her finger and demanded that he "stop that and be quiet." At least, that was my best guess at her words, which weren't English. She sounded a lot like our Ukrainian neighbour telling her son, Fred, to stop playing and come in for supper.

I glimpsed John pulling his hand out of his right jacket pocket. He put something in his mouth. "What are you eating?"

"Oh, here." He withdrew a crumpled paper sack from the same pocket. "I forgot. Papa said to give these to you." Inside were three butterscotch candies. When he fished his own bag from the other pocket, it bulged. How many of mine had he eaten?

As the train steamed along, the car swayed from side to side. I sucked a candy and watched the birch and fir trees whip past. Often the forest was too thick with evergreens to see through to Lake Superior. The occasional flash of glittering blue water kept me hoping to see more. How exciting it was to be so far from home!

A few miles past Red Rock, the tracks squeezed between a high mountain and the lake. There were no trees on the lake side, only telegraph poles and rocks.

The whistle shrieked through the morning stillness as we arrived in Nipigon. The train wheezed to a stop in front of the long CPR building. Storefronts and hotels lined the far side of the town's main street.

Two sturdy men boarded the Colonist car, shouting, *"Au revoir!"* to their friends. Marching up the aisle with their bags held overhead, they smelled of newly cut wood.

The train lurched into motion. Before I could ask Mama for a sandwich, I heard the man behind us tell his companion, "Keep looking. It's coming up in a moment."

I pressed my forehead to the glass so I wouldn't miss "it," whatever "it" turned out to be.

"They used wooden trestles at first," he said, "but then masonry and steel to build…"

The ground disappeared. Swirling white water lay far below where I sat.

"…the Nipigon River bridge."

The lumberjacks stood at their window, exclaimed in French, and pointed down at the narrow rapids.

"John, come quickly." I pulled him in front of me. We stared at the hundreds of logs freely tumbling and colliding in the river's strong current.

Past the bridge, a thick forest of spruce, balsam, and pine trees closed in. Soon the novelty of trees wore off, and the gnawing in my stomach grew. Mama unwrapped a parcel of sandwiches that Mrs. Pekkonen had brought over early in the morning. Generous slices of meat were stuffed between buttered dark rye bread. Lately, we could afford to have meat only a few times a week. John and I tore into our meal.

"We'll save our *pulla* for coffee time," said Mama, opening a quart sealer of water for a drink.

In our train car, men read newspapers or played cards, while ladies did handwork or read books. Mama's knitting needles clicked as she fashioned a sweater for Auntie's baby. John wandered down the aisle and stopped to chat with two salesmen in the last pair of seats.

I munched the rest of my sandwich while staring at the blue water that stretched as far as my eyes could see. Ripples sparkled and danced as they caught the sun. After more than two hours of rattling along in the train, the tracks still hugged the shore of the same Great Lake. It was a rugged land with dense forests, sheer cliffs, and enormous boulders speckled with orange lichen.

Unexpectedly, a solid granite wall appeared and we were swallowed into a dark hole. When the train emerged from the tunnel, the sunlight blinded me for a moment, then I gasped.

"What?" asked Mama.

"It feels as if the train will tumble into the lake."

Mama smiled. "I know. But remember, trains cross this route safely every day—in both directions."

The coach swayed. The train's front half snaked around a curve. I could see the swath of black smoke billowing out of the stack and over the top of the locomotive, tender, mail car, and baggage car. As we approached a cluster of wooden buildings, the whistle blew.

John dashed back waving a deck of playing cards. "One of the salesmen let me borrow these so do you want to play a game, Saara?"

"Okay."

John fumbled with the deck trying to shuffle, dropping several cards between the slats of the seat. Shifting on the hard bench, I asked, "Mama, may we please sit on the blanket?"

"Of course you may," she said, reaching for a bag. "Papa was right about these seats."

John's card dealing was painfully slow. I tapped my foot in time with the train: *one*, two, three, four, *one*, two, three, four, willing him to move faster.

"Stop that racket, Saara," said Mama. "The train doesn't need your help to fill our ears with clatter."

I trounced my brother. John huffed and threw down his cards. I gathered the lot and shuffled.

"Let's play Beggar-My-Neighbour instead," he said. "I have a chance of winning that."

We were still playing the first game when the conductor announced a ten-minute stop in Schreiber. Mama said, "Let's go stretch our legs."

The train shuddered and squealed to a halt. Most people stepped down to the ground to pace the length of the train. I hadn't noticed how stuffy it had gotten inside the train car until I breathed fresh air. A few men, their tapered suits and bowlers declaring first class, joined us outside.

Back in our seats, I wrinkled my nose at the stale

odours. The temperature rose.

"What do you want to play?" asked John. "X's and O's?"

"All right. We can use the back page of my journal." Seeing the smooth leather cover of Helena's gift, I felt a spasm of resentment over the way she'd treated me at our farewell supper.

"I want X's," said John. Soon our games filled three-quarters of the page.

Mama exclaimed at the view, luring us to the soot-edged window. The CPR's rails hugged the shoreline of a bay and tunnelled through a solid rock cliff.

"That's Jackfish," stated the man seated behind us. "Most expensive mile of track this side of the Rockies."

"Saara, will you play some more?" begged John.

If only there were some other children his age for him to hound. "Two more. Then I want to read."

John lost both and pouted when I clapped my journal shut. Finding *Black Beauty*, I wriggled around trying to get comfortable. Mama leaned against the window, eyes closed. After reading several pages, I yawned. The train car grew unpleasantly warm and smelled of sweaty bodies. I lasted another page before dozing off.

I woke to the aroma of a passenger's coffee brewing on the pot-bellied stove.

"That makes me wish I'd brought my own coffee pot and supplies," said Mama, yawning. "Would you like some *pulla* now?"

I nodded and breathed in the sweet cardamom scent before taking a bite. John interrupted his solitaire game to stuff a slice of *pulla* in his mouth and grab another.

Through the blanket, the slats pressed hard into my backside. I squirmed. Outside, the poplars were tinged green. Mile after mile the train rolled past rocks, forests, and small lakes. Occasionally we'd have a breathtaking view of Lake Superior, its cobble beaches strewn with tree-trunk driftwood. All that Mr. McKee had taught us about the CPR's construction through the wilderness came alive. It was a feat as impressive as he'd claimed. I wondered what the animals thought of the noisy black "beast" screaming through their homeland.

My journal's blank pages beckoned. Flinging back my braids, I wrote:

Tuesday, May 26, 1914
I can't believe I am really on the train and I will be in Montreal tomorrow. If only my brother the PEST wasn't along, it would be perfect. I wish I had a pillow to sit on. I can't say that to Mama. She would give me her "be thankful for what you have" speech and remind me that we're fortunate to be on this trip at all.

We slowed down to cross an extremely high bridge over a cascading river. Now it is back to rocks, trees, rocks, trees. Will this province ever end?

I closed my journal, stood up, and stretched my arms over my head.

"Could you read to me, Saara?" asked John, pleading with his whole bored body. I agreed and introduced him to the world as seen by a beautiful black horse.

Later, I wrote:

105

It is getting dark outside and the ceiling lamps are shining. Before I climb into the upper berth I want to write what I saw. I thought it was a tree with antler-shaped branches beside a pond. But the tree began to walk away! It was a bull moose!

I wish I had a mattress. I will be miserable with only my coat between the hard wood and me.

Mama and John shared the lower berth, with their heads at opposite ends. Once I got used to the clickety-clack of the train, the snoring and coughing of other passengers kept me awake. Finally I drifted off, only to be startled by the terrifying noise of another train rushing past. It took forever to fall asleep again.

Screech! The train stopped in the dark. A deep voice said, "Ladies and gentlemen, my apologies for disturbing your sleep." The lamps blazed. "A forest fire has burned the trestle bridge ahead."

When I explained the announcement to Mama, she moaned, "Our trip is over."

"CPR crews have begun repairs," he continued, "but you will need to transfer to a train on the other side. Please gather your belongings and exit the train. Watch your step!"

Outside, the air stank of scorched creosoted wood and burnt trees. The brittle grass crunched underfoot as we followed a lantern-bearing trainman.

There was a commotion next to a first-class car. An old lady refused to move, saying, "I paid my fare to ride a train, not to walk through a putrid ravine."

One of the workmen spewed a stream of cusses, then picked her up and carried her down the hill. She flailed and sputtered the whole way.

We were assigned to a Tourist coach with soft leather seats and, best of all, mattresses.

Wednesday, May 27, 1914, late afternoon
I had a heavenly sleep last night once the train finally got under way. We will be late getting to Montreal. See how neat my handwriting is? Each pair of seats shares a table, so no more writing on my lap. I miss Lake Superior. This part of the route is flat, the rivers sluggish. The trees are beautiful, though, dressed in their new leaves.

John's stomach growled loudly enough for the people around us to hear. "Mama, what can I eat?"

"Have a sandwich."

He took a bite and spat it out. "It tastes bad."

Mama sniffed the filling. "Oh! It's spoiled. Have a carrot or *näkkileipä* or *pulla*." He and I both selected a slice of the sweet bread.

The conductor, in his spotless uniform, boomed, "CHALK RIVER NEXT STOP!"

The three-day-old *pulla* was dry as chalk in my mouth. I wished for butter to help it slide down. Helena's mother always told me to put more butter on my... It hurt to think about being at Helena's house.

John gagged on his huge bite. "We need coffee to dunk it in."

"Here, have a drink of water," said Mama, passing him the jar I had refilled at the lavatory faucet. "The moment we walk into my mother's house she'll have us sit down. There will be coffee with cream and fresh-baked *pulla*, and cookies, and—" Her hand flew to her mouth. "What am I saying? She's too sick to be baking."

The most recent letter from Finland had said my bedridden grandmother had worsened. A gloomy silence blanketed us as the train chugged eastward toward Montreal.

"Pardon me," said the young woman in the seat ahead of us. "Would you like some of our sandwiches?" She had boarded the train with her husband and rosy-cheeked baby in North Bay. "We have more than we could possibly eat." She offered us the food. Mama smiled and shook her head.

"Please may I have some, Mama? I'm starving." John hugged himself and groaned.

"We have enough to last—" said Mama.

"But I choked on the *pulla*. A piece of *näkkileipä* would be worse. And I've already eaten three carrots. Please?"

"You may have a little," she said, "and mind your manners." Turning to face the lady, she said in English, "You are good person," then dipped her head in thanks.

With moist ham and cheese sandwiches and juicy apples filling our bellies, John and I fell asleep. Mama shook us awake just before we arrived at Windsor Station in Montreal. John was so groggy we needed to help him off the train. After asking for directions, we walked to the Queen's Hotel. I caught the scent of a blooming lilac bush nearby, and the cool air perked me up. Still, I could hardly wait to climb into a regular bed.

11

A jumble of morning street noises woke me up. Automobile horns, hooves striking cobblestones, "...*pain frais du jour...*," "VIOLENT STORM AFTER HEAT WAVE! ONE MAN KILLED BY LIGHTNING! READ ALL ABOUT IT!" After two days of constant rolling and swaying along the CPR rails it felt strange to lie in a motionless bed. Turning on my side, I could see Mama and John sleeping.

Moving as quietly as Sipu, I padded across the room to peek at Montreal in daylight. In Port Arthur, the brand-new eight-storey Whalen building was the only one that tall. Before me stood several such buildings. There were more people outside already than I was used to seeing in a whole day. A newsboy, not much bigger than John, lugged an armful of newspapers. The aroma of freshly baked bread mingled with gasoline exhaust fumes from the black Model T motor cars.

"Good morning, Sunshine," said Mama, her voice drowsy.

"Mama, come and see. The city goes on forever."

John sat up and rubbed his eyes. "Do we *have* to go on another train right away? I want to play in a park. *Please?*"

"I'd like to see inside those big stores," I said.

"This morning we must catch the train to the city of Quebec or we'll miss our sailing time."

We took turns using the shared lavatory down the hall and dressed for the day. Mama insisted that we wear our Sunday clothes. On my braids she even tied ribbons that matched my new blue dress. Within an hour we were enjoying our French bread and cheese picnic breakfast on board the *Empress Special*. What a relief to know this train trip would be a short few hours.

The coach was packed with adults, mainly men. Several wore dark blue uniforms. Their tunics had high collars with an "S" on each side. As the train moved forward, John inspected the passengers gently swaying in their seats.

The man across the aisle met his stare. He leaned over, saying, "Good mornin', lad."

Wide-eyed, John asked, "Are you a soldier?"

"Only in the army of the Lord, sonny," answered the grey-haired gentleman in a kind voice.

"Do you have guns and cannons?"

"Just the sword of the Spirit, lad, God's mighty word, the Bible."

"George," said the matronly woman by the window, "I believe this young boy has never met a Salvation Army soldier before." She wore an ankle-length, dark blue belted dress, with the same type of high collar as the man. "This is my husband, Major Parker, and I'm Mrs. Parker."

"I'm John."

"Where is your home, dearie?"

"Port Arthur, ma'am, in New Ontario. We've been on a train for two days already. There are people like you back home, but my father warned me to stay away from them."

"John!" I cringed. "All Papa said was that they do things differently than in our church." Feeling my cheeks flare, I turned to look at the rolling hills and spring-green woods outside.

"Oh, I understand," said Major Parker, chuckling. "I've heard that folks in your community think preaching on a street corner is odd, but we mean no harm." His friendliness set me at ease.

"We're going to Finland," bragged John. "Where are you going?"

"To London, for our International Congress. Many of our group are bandsmen in the Canadian Salvation Army Staff Band." He waved his arm to indicate uniformed passengers in our coach and those in more train cars ahead. "There are almost two hundred of us going from Canada alone."

"Golly, that's like having our whole church go on a trip."

"Jussi, stop bothering the man," cautioned Mama, glancing nervously at the uniformed couple.

"That's a language new to me," said Major Parker.

"Can't say I've ever heard anything like it. Does your mother think you are disturbing me?"

"Yes, sir."

"Well, don't you worry, sonny. If God puts a lad next to me and he wants to talk, there's a reason. Ask me anything you like."

At his invitation, I blurted the questions stacked up in *my* head. "Why are you called an army? Do girls and boys wear uniforms too? Do you have—"

"Whoa, slow down, young lady. This antique brain can't go too quick anymore." Major Parker settled back in his seat. "Years ago, in London, William Booth started a Christian mission to the poor to preach God's love and salvation. Later on he renamed it the Salvation Army. We're soldiers in a spiritual war, fighting sin and battling for people's souls."

"Are there children in your church?" asked John.

"Oh, yes," said Mrs. Parker. "And the children who profess their belief in Jesus are called Junior Soldiers."

Our conversation carried on, made even more enjoyable with peppermints and maple sweets from Mrs. Parker. They asked us about life in Port Arthur. Occasionally I looked out at the passing views of long, narrow farmlands stretching back from the St. Lawrence River. Mama drank in the scenery with a dreamy expression on her face. After the train passed Three Rivers, Major Parker entertained John with adventures of his youth in England and I buried my nose in my book.

How surprising it was to hear the conductor announce our destination. Through the windows of the coach I saw a hodgepodge of brick and stone buildings, new and old. The train slowed as it approached the pier below the old section of Quebec. Narrow lanes wound their way uphill to the ancient city walls. Crowds of travellers and well-wishers had already gathered, while porters struggled to manhandle piles of trunks and cases.

"'Tis a marvel how the drivers of the calèches keep their horses safe in this bedlam," said Mrs. Parker. Several of the two-wheeled buggies snaked their way around the taxis and through the waves of pedestrians.

Mama collected our belongings. "Saara, Jussi, stay close to me. I don't want to lose you in this beehive." I expected to see her usual do-as-I-say look. To my amazement, there was an excited twinkle in Mama's eye. The long-awaited voyage would soon begin.

We said farewell to the Parkers and stepped off the train into a jostling, noisy throng. Mama, lugging the large suitcase and a bag, joined the flow of ship-bound passengers. We followed, John toting a cloth bag slung over his shoulder while I carried the smaller suitcase.

"Wait, Saara, my bootlace is undone," called John.

"Hurry." I stood on my tiptoes to track Mama's head topped with her new straw hat. Grasping John's hand, I said, "Forget your lace. We must keep up."

A finely dressed couple emerged from the train and passed right in front of us. The brilliant greens and blues of the peacock feather in the lady's hat flashed in the sunlight. Her dress of matching green silk billowed and shone, rustling like poplar leaves in a strong breeze. The gentleman wore an overcoat with a fur collar and an opera cape. Pausing, the lady smiled up at his intense dark eyes and reached to adjust the silk scarf around his neck.

"Stop gawking," said John, pulling me along in pursuit of Mama. I focused on our mother's hat with its bright blue trim as we wove through the crowd.

All at once John and I stopped in our tracks, staring at the immense black hull of the ship docked up ahead. I recognized the *Empress of Ireland* from the brochure I'd picked up in Port Arthur, but it hadn't prepared me for seeing the real thing. I felt like an ant approaching a mountain. Above the row of brown lifeboats towered the ship's two buff-coloured funnels that angled backwards. Strands of smoke curled upward from their black tops. High on the mast at the back of the steamer fluttered a red and white checkered flag. The ship's steam winches hoisted large trunks and cargo on board. Passengers stood at the rails of the open decks looking down at the frenzy on the pier.

"Oh, no!" yelled John, jerking my arm. "I can't see Mama anymore. What do we do?"

I scanned the sea of hats, telling myself not to panic. "Let's ask that man in the uniform for directions."

From behind, he looked like a CPR official. However, we soon realized he was another Salvation Army soldier.

"Ask him anyway, Saara."

"All right. I beg your pardon, sir. Can you please tell us how to get to the third-class boarding area?"

"I'm a Salvationist, not a steward, but I certainly can. Follow us. We're heading that way ourselves." The "us" he spoke of included a woman and a girl about ten years old. The girl had dark brown curly hair fastened with yellow bows on either side of her head.

It didn't take long to locate the correct spot on the wharf. What a relief to see Mama's new headgear bobbing up and down, and to hear her frantically calling our names. As she clutched both of us, she whispered, "Thank you, Father in Heaven. You two gave me such a fright."

"Keep out of the stevedore's way, son," said the Salvationist, drawing John aside. A man with bulging muscles grunted as he wheeled a barrow of luggage to the gangway. From there the baggage was loaded by hand onto the boat. Four decks of the ship rose high above the entrance for third-class passengers.

When I stepped onto the gangway, I was no longer a plain daughter of immigrants. I was a princess crossing the drawbridge, with crocodiles snapping in the moat below. The ship's flags were my regal banners, the crowd my loyal subjects, and my homemade dress a gown of shimmering jewels. Once on board, or rather, inside my floating palace, I continued the delectable fantasy.

"Ouch! Get off my foot, Saara," said John.

"Attach this tag, Saara," said Mama, "while I get my bearings."

My world of monarchy evaporated. I blinked several times, then tied the "UNWANTED" tag on the big suitcase containing summer clothing heading to the storage hold. My nose twitched at the smell of oranges and fish.

"We need to find our cabin," said Mama.

"I'll carry the suitcase," offered John.

"Thank you, Jussi, but I'll take it. Your sister's books make it extra heavy. You can each take a bag."

I studied our surroundings along the way. The ship was more elaborately built than I'd imagined. Exotic wood had been used for the passageway floor and for the walls in the third-class ladies' social hall. I could hardly comprehend how first class topped that. Maybe it had marble, like the lobby of the Whalen building back home.

Mama glanced around, looking confused. "There's a steward, Saara, with the shiny black hair and blue jacket. Ask him for directions."

The crew member explained the ship's layout to me.

"Mama, we have to go down to Main Deck." I took the lead down a steep stairway into the third-class quarters. The steady beat of the ship's engines grew louder. In the congested, well-lit corridor I felt as if we were back home walking along Bay Street with its mix of nationalities. My ears buzzed with snatches of Hungarian, Finnish, and Italian.

"How much farther?" asked John.

I shrugged.

"I wish I could see outside. Are we below water level? Do we have to sleep on the bottom of the boat?"

Mama groaned. "Jussi, hush."

I read the numbers on the next cabin location sign. "It should be close." If I were a princess, I would have been escorted to my luxury accommodation on the uppermost deck and I certainly would not have carried my own luggage. "Here it is."

The door to the tiny inside cabin was ajar and spirited humming drifted into the hallway. A stewardess bustled about placing folded sheets from the stack on her arm onto the berths.

"Aw, gee, no window," muttered John.

"Hello," I said.

"Oh, hello. I'm sorry. I've been so busy your cabin is not ready." She wore a navy blue serge uniform, muslin apron, and a sunny smile. "Madam, let me take your suitcase. Such sweet darlings," said the woman, patting us on our heads. John ducked, but too late.

"I have a grand idea," she continued. "On Upper Deck, next to where you boarded, there is a large sandpit. The children will enjoy playing there."

I translated for Mama and frowned. I hadn't played in a sandpit since I was six.

"Let's go there," said John. His face became serious as he turned to the stewardess. "Where is my lifebelt? I can't swim."

She checked the overhead rack. "You'll be needing a children's size. I'll fetch one from storage and leave it on the berth." She patted John's head again. "Off you go," she said, shooing us away. "I shan't be long. When you come back, everything will be ready. Ta-ra now, darlings."

"If the beds were made I'd lie down," said Mama with a heavy sigh. "Come on, we had better let the woman get her work done."

"Hurrah! I can't wait to see the sky," said John. I was eager to explore the *Empress*. Mama trudged along behind.

117

"Hello, again." It was the Salvationist who had helped us find Mama on the pier. "Follow us. We're going up to Shelter Deck for departure." Thank goodness he knew his way around the gigantic ship. Once we reached the open deck at the stern of the *Empress*, we saw that passengers were still embarking, joining the hundreds on board.

"Golly, look at that castle." John pointed to the Château Frontenac perched high on the cliff, complete with turrets. "I wish I could live there. Do you suppose there are any secret passageways?"

"Yes, John," I said. "Dumbwaiters and laundry chutes. It's a CPR hotel, don't you know?" He stuck his tongue out at me.

Beyond the city lay the bluish silhouette of mountains. A smaller community spread over the bank of the St. Lawrence River directly opposite the Château.

Our "guide" and his family posed along the rail. "Make certain the Château Frontenac gets in the background," he called to the man aiming a Kodak Brownie camera. *Click.*

"Wait one moment, please. Young lady. Yes, you with the golden braids. Bring your mother and brother for a photograph with us."

Mama shook her head when John explained, so he left her side to join the group with me. *Click.*

"Take one more." *Click.*

"We must introduce ourselves," he said, holding out his right hand. "Mr. Blackwell, and my wife, Mrs. Blackwell, and Lucy-Jane."

"I'm Saara, this is John, and our mother, Mrs. Mäki."

"Very pleased to meet you. May I have your address in order to send you one of these snapshots?" I gave the information while Mr. Blackwell wrote in a small notebook. "Foley Street. Foley is my mother's family name. What is your destination?"

"Finland, sir, to visit our relatives there. Are you going to London?"

"Ah, so you've already learned of our International Congress. We shall also visit our relatives so they can meet our baby."

Baby? Did he mean Lucy-Jane? Perhaps she was going to see her grandparents for the first time, too.

A lady next to me exclaimed to her neighbour, "It *is* the Irvings. Can you believe our luck being on the same boat as that famous pair?"

I hunted in the direction she pointed, and saw a familiar peacock feather two decks above. I'd been close enough to touch actress Mabel Hackney and hadn't known it. She clung with one arm to her dignified actor husband, Laurence Irving, and waved with the other to their admirers onshore.

A bugle call rang out, followed by the stewards chanting, "All ashore that's going ashore!"

"We're about to set sail," said Mr. Blackwell, inhaling deeply. "A fine evening for a cruise."

Over on the first-class gangway an orange tabby cat headed to the pier, darting around oncoming legs.

"Emmy's jumping ship," called a nearby steward, pointing to the cat. No wonder. Sipu would have hated the confusion. The sight of Emmy ignited a pang of

119

longing in me. I wanted to scoop up my cat for a cuddle.

One of the crew caught Emmy and carried her back on board. Why hadn't she found a safe place to hide on the ship? No sooner had the man put her down than she scrambled up on the rail and leaped to her escape route again.

The steward shook his head. "Emmy's been our ship's mascot for years and hasn't left us before." A shiver ran through me as I saw Emmy reach the wharf and slip into a freight shed.

From a higher deck, a lady called out, "Goodbye and God bless you."

In reply from land came, "Godspeed, my love. I'll not rest well 'til you return."

As the crew stowed the third-class gangway, we heard the familiar notes of "O Canada."

"Look, our Staff Band has assembled," said Mr. Blackwell.

"My," said Mrs. Blackwell, "aren't they smart in their made-for-Congress uniforms."

The bandsmen, in their scarlet tunics and stetson hats, could have passed for Royal North West Mounted Police. Next they played "Auld Lang Syne." Black smoke spewed from the ship's funnels as we eased away from the pier. We were under way at last!

The bandsmen began a farewell hymn. Lucy-Jane's mother softly sang, "*God be with you till we meet again, by His counsels guide, uphold you—*"

The deep blast of the ship's steam whistle drowned out every other sound.

Those gathered onshore cheered and waved handkerchiefs, hats, hands, and tiny Union Jacks. The whistle blew again.

As singing reached my ears I heard, *"When life's perils thick confound you, put His loving arms around you..."*

I stared at Lucy-Jane with her father's arm around her. He looked so proud of his daughter. Papa used to be proud of me, like when I recited "The Sleeping Giant." We'd been out of sorts for so long I could hardly remember anything different. When we were leaving Port Arthur he had seemed pleased with my help in the library. My insides squirmed at how I'd dashed onto the train without saying goodbye. A tear slid down my face. I wiped it away with the back of my hand. I missed Papa. It felt as though months had passed since we'd parted, instead of days.

Mr. Blackwell leaned his head in my direction, opened his mouth to speak, and simply smiled. His eyes shone with concern.

The singing grew louder as more voices joined in. *"Keep love's banner floating o'er you, smite death's threatening wave..."*

Death's wave? I didn't like the sound of that, being on a boat. At least we were safe on such a massive ship. No wave could get high enough to hurt us here.

"God be with you till we meet again."

Bold notes burst forth from the shining silver instruments as the bandsmen concluded the hymn. We waved to the crowd onshore while the gap between pier and ship widened. I thought I saw a small orange animal on the wharf. *Goodbye, Emmy.*

Mr. Blackwell, hugging his daughter in front of him, closed his eyes. "Our Father in Heaven, we commit this voyage to Thee and we ask for safety from Thy hand of mercy. May we be faithful in our service to Thee. Amen."

I didn't know if it was the man's deep, sincere voice, or the way he spoke to God as if He were a good friend, but as he prayed a warm calm filled me, like a cup of hot cocoa on a January day.

12

The *Empress of Ireland* sailed between an island on the right and the rugged shoreline to the left.

Lucy-Jane tugged on her mother's sleeve. "Mum, may I please go to the playground now?"

"Mama, can I go play, too?" echoed John. Both mothers gave their permission.

I wanted to stay on the open deck, but I didn't want to walk forward through the long maze of corridors on my own. Not that Mama would let me.

We all set off. Eventually we reached the third-class indoor children's playground. A dozen or so children scooped and piled sand in the huge play area enclosed by a wooden fence.

John's eyes widened. "This is bully!" He raced Lucy-Jane around the corner where they ducked through the gate. The bars of the fence were shaped like Union Jacks standing on end. I slouched on a slatted wooden bench next to Mama.

"Are you going to play?" she asked.

"No. A sandpit is far too childish."

Mama gave me an odd look, then smiled. I turned away to watch the childish activity. Squatting, Lucy-Jane smoothed rectangular patches and traced around them with her fingers. Inside the flattened areas she set down tiny clumps in a haphazard arrangement.

"Saara, come join me," she said. "The sand is splendid."

"Well... all right." I shuffled into the playground. "What are you making?"

"Farms here, and a city over there. It will have a park in the centre with a lake and ducks and rowboats," she said, her words tumbling out like a waterfall. "The farms have lots of goats and chickens."

"With horses and cows?"

"Yes, and sheep—"

"And dogs—"

"And cats—"

"Can I play with you?" asked John.

I grimaced, wishing he'd find some boys for his war games.

"Yes," replied Lucy-Jane. "The more, the merrier, as my father says."

"No." I bristled. "There aren't any soldiers or castles."

"That doesn't matter."

"Besides, you aren't careful enough."

"I am so!"

"London has castles," offered Lucy-Jane. "My father told me."

"I'm tired of playing with my brother. It's all I've done

for three days on the train. John, go somewhere else." The hurt look on his face pricked my conscience, but I didn't back down. He kicked the sand, spraying my legs, before running to the other end of the sandpit.

"Good riddance," I muttered.

Less than five minutes later Mama called me to the fence. "This is my daughter, Saara," she said to the woman with upswept blond hair beside her. "Saara, this is Mrs. Simola. She is travelling to Finland, too. We're going to the ladies' social room next door to find some comfortable chairs. I want you to mind Jussi."

With gritted teeth, I managed to squeeze out, "Yes, Mama."

When John heard Mama's plan he trotted over to me, grinning from ear to ear. "Ha, ha. Now you *have* to let me play."

"Don't you dare wreck anything."

I was relieved when he joined in that he didn't want to change everything into a battle scene. He could be pleasant when he tried.

Once Lucy-Jane finished pinching bits of sand to form ducks on her lake, she pointed to the *Empress*'s windows. "Do you know why portholes are round?"

I thought for a few seconds. "No, why?"

"So that when the water comes in," she replied, smiling, "it won't hit you square in the face." Lucy-Jane collapsed with giggles and John laughed. I groaned and returned to heaping sand in a ridge of mountains along the edge of the horses' pasture.

"Oh my," said a lady's voice from behind me, "how

delightful to see children frolicking in a playground."

I glanced over at an elegant couple in the doorway. The gentleman adjusted his hat and stroked his walrus moustache. "We have definitely made a wrong turn, dearest. This is hardly the place to mail our postcards."

As the pair came alongside us, the lady cooed to her partner, "Darling, did you notice those velvet chairs in the library? Oh, do let's go and relax there before we dine."

"But we must allow ourselves time to get ready for—"

"Have you forgotten? There is no need to dress for dinner on the first night out."

Lucy-Jane's eyes grew large. She whispered, "Can you picture all those rich folks sitting down to eat with nothing on?"

John snickered.

"She meant no need to dress *up*," I said, "to change into evening—" The expression on Lucy-Jane's face told me she knew full well what the lady had meant. John slapped his leg and guffawed.

"It's a funny sight to imagine, isn't it?" said Lucy-Jane with a wink.

Still irked by my brother, I gave her a weak smile. My time on board the *Empress* would be anything but dull with my spunky new friend.

"Yoo-hoo! Lucy-Jane," sang Mrs. Blackwell. "Time for tea."

When I jumped up, my head tingled and I felt dizzy. Tea? Only tea? I needed to eat. Mama and Mrs. Simola returned from their visit and we joined the stream of passengers going below to Main Deck. Cabin doors opened on our way to add more adults and children to the crowded corridor.

Lucy-Jane linked her arm in mine. "I'm so glad to have a chum."

"Me, too." It had been months since I'd walked like that with Helena.

"Let's play in the sandpit again tomorrow, all right?" Bouncing curls surrounded her cheerful face. I nodded, grinning. "Would you like to come to my cabin after tea to play a game? I have Parcheesi and Snakes and Ladders."

"I'd like that, Lucy-Jane."

"I prefer Snakes and Ladders—my version. After you slide down a snake, if you roll a three or less you have to stay there for another turn." With saucer eyes she gave a quiet but slightly wicked laugh and whispered, "It's like the snake coils around you—"

"Uh… Parcheesi is my favourite, traditional rules."

"Oh, really?" Lucy-Jane shrugged. "Any game is fine with me."

"Not much farther," said Mr. Blackwell. "The third-class dining saloon is amidships, between the two funnels." With his dark blue Salvation Army uniform, he looked and behaved like a ship's steward conducting a tour.

The aroma of freshly brewed coffee welcomed us to the dining room. White tablecloths covered the tables. There was space for over three hundred passengers to dine. I peeked through a porthole at a village glowing in evening sunlight, with a wall of mountains rising in the distance.

"In about one hour we'll pass Cap Tourmente." Mr. Blackwell's deep voice rumbled beside me. "Its volcanic rock is most impressive."

"Saara," called Lucy-Jane. "Come sit with me."

I sat down between her and Mama, who talked non-stop with Mrs. Simola beside her. The stewards set platters of food before us. I filled my plate with cold meats, pickles, bread, and jam, and skipped the smoked herring. Using my fork I stabbed a pickle. With it at my mouth, I noticed Mrs. Blackwell frowning at me. Lucy-Jane's father asked, "Shall I say grace for our table?" I lowered my fork and bowed my head.

"Heavenly Father, I ask that Thou would bless this food to us Thy children, and I thank Thee for these new acquaintances with whom to share this meal. Amen."

"Mr. Blackwell," said John, seated next to him, "I know what 'RMS' in front of *Empress of Ireland* means."

"And what would that be, Master John?"

"Really Modern Ship."

Mr. Blackwell chuckled. "Clever lad. The letters actually stand for 'Royal Mail Steamer.'" John's smile faded. "During the second watch of the night, the *Empress* will meet up with the vessel *Lady Evelyn* near Rimouski and exchange bags of mail."

"Pass the meat, please, dear."

He handed the platter to his wife and said, "On my first voyage aboard the *Empress*, I waited up to watch the exchange. Even later, I observed the river pilot transfer to a small boat to be ferried to Father Point. He had guided the steamship through the dangerous sections of the St. Lawrence."

"What time will the pilot get off?"

"During the second, or middle, watch, around two o'clock in the morning. The first watch is eight o'clock to midnight and the second watch is midnight to four in the morning."

In a rush John translated to Mama what Lucy-Jane's father had described and asked if he could stay up to see the events.

Mama shook her head. "Certainly not. That is far too late for a young boy to be awake."

The "young boy" pouted.

Mr. Blackwell cleared his throat. "John, did you know that it takes five days to load the coal this ship requires?" He was either not hungry or he loved to talk about the *Empress of Ireland*. He droned on. "…twin-screw quadruple-expansion engines…"

I felt and heard the throbbing pulse of the engines above the clinking of cutlery and the chattering of diners. My brother listened to, and likely memorized, every piece of trivia about the ship.

"…full speed at eighteen to twenty knots."

"Pardon me," I said, "what time is breakfast tomorrow?" At least that was a practical piece of information we needed to know.

"At eight o'clock, Saara. Now, where was I? Oh yes, safety features. The *Empress of Ireland* and her sister ship, the *Empress of Britain,* are the most reliable steamers in their class and—"

"I don't believe any boat is totally safe," interrupted the slight woman at the end of the table.

"Pshaw. This ship had no faults whatsoever on her recent safety inspection," said Mr. Blackwell. "The *Empress* has carried me to England and back three times without incident."

"Ach, but what of the habit of captains drinking liquor?" she asked.

"Captain Kendall never drinks. He's a rigid teetotaller."

"Pardon me, sir," said John, "when the captain orders a change in speed, how do the firemen know how much coal to shovel into the furnace?"

I raised my hand to stifle a yawn. My head felt fuzzy inside, as if it were stuffed with cotton batting. I crumbled a piece of bread and licked jam off my fingers. My stomach felt unsettled. Would my brother never run out of questions?

"Have you had enough, Miss?" asked a steward, reaching for my plate.

Conversation swirled around my ears like autumn leaves in an eddy of wind. I lost my concentration. I wanted to lie down and shut out the world. How frustrating. I was finally on the *Empress* and all I could think about was sleeping.

"Saara, your cheeks are flushed," said Mama, her brow creased. "Are you unwell?"

"I'm so tired, Mama. Could we go to our cabin?"

"Yes, of course. It has been a long day. Come, Jussi."

I stood. "See you tomorrow, Lucy-Jane. We'll play a game in the morning, all right?"

She nodded, bright-eyed. "Good night, chum. Sleep well."

Mama said goodbye to Mrs. Simola. She turned to the Blackwells. "We go. Good night."

For once Mama's faltering English didn't embarrass me. I was grateful to escape the crowded room. There was so much to write in my journal, but it would have to wait until morning. In our cabin, I lay down on one of the straw mattresses right away. Mama unlaced and removed my boots, then tucked a blanket around me.

"Do *I* have to go to bed already?" said John. "I'm not sleepy. Can we go explore?" I couldn't believe how much energy he still had.

"Yes, Jussi," said Mama. "Saara, we won't be gone long."

Yawning, I said, "That's fine."

A queasy churning in my belly woke me. I blinked and squinted in the dark, hearing rhythmic breathing from the other berths.

"Mama? Mama!"

"What?"

"I'm going to be sick to my stomach."

Mama held my arm and rushed me along the vacant passageway to the lavatory.

When I came out I felt a bit better. The few hours of sleep had eased my dizziness. "How can I be seasick? I can hardly feel the boat moving."

"You might have influenza, or you ate something bad." Mama placed her cool palm on my forehead. "No fever. Let's go up to the open deck. Some fresh air will help. But first I'll check on Jussi."

My brother was sleeping like a bear in winter. We put on our coats and boots. After closing the cabin door Mama said, "He looks ridiculous wearing his lifebelt in bed, but he insisted." She drew a handkerchief out of her handbag. "Hold this over your mouth. My poor girl." Her sympathy and her arm wrapped around me like a shawl. I didn't mind being babied. With her free hand Mama gathered the skirt of her nightdress for climbing the steps.

Standing at the right-side rail toward the bow, I shivered from the bite of the spring air. Three more decks towered above us. I recalled my dream from the day we purchased our tickets. In it, I stood at a similar ship's rail, but the sun was bright and I felt glorious. On the *Empress,* the electric lights shone, and I felt the urge to retch again. I leaned over the side. The calm, black water was a long way down, like to the street from three storeys up. I was relieved that no one else was around.

Clank. Mortified, I turned and saw a crewman near the opposite rail, his back to us, washing the deck. With my ears tuned for noises I realized that the ship's engines were silent.

Moments later, a small boat came into view, pulling away from the *Empress.* Based on what Lucy-Jane's father had said, the boat was carrying the mail or the river pilot. That meant it was well after midnight.

The engines of the *Empress* sprang to life. As the steamship gained speed, I looked across the bow and noticed that the St. Lawrence had grown much wider.

"Oh, Mama. What a way to start our voyage. I hope I'm well by Saturday when we reach open sea."

"There, there, child. 'We live as we can, not as we may wish.' We will deal with whatever comes." I snuggled closer to my mother.

The peace was broken by the sharp clang of a bell, startling us both. The bell sounded a second time, followed by a shout. "Object to starboard!"

The lights of a ship blinked in the distance to the right. Was it coming toward us or were we catching up to it? Before the mystery could be solved, the lights disappeared. But so did the shore lights. We were suddenly surrounded by fog.

With Mama's arm around me, I felt her tremble. "How are you now?" she asked.

"A little better," I said, despite being chilled by the damp air.

"Let's go back to bed."

"Could we stay a few more minutes?" I couldn't face being cooped up in our cabin yet. A crewman carrying a rope ladder tipped his cap as he passed us.

The deck shuddered as the *Empress* slowed. The whistle blew three short blasts and the ship started going backwards. I couldn't remember Mr. Blackwell saying anything about reversing direction.

A single long blast drifted through the wall of fog— from where, it was impossible to say. My eardrums rang from the volley of shrill whistles. The *Empress* stopped, sounding two long blasts. Where was that other ship? It gave another long signal, followed by two more blasts from the *Empress*.

On the deck below us, a man stuck his head out of a porthole and asked, "What's the racket about?"

I sucked in a breath. "Look! The lights are closer!"

Out of the mist emerged a large black boat. It rode low in the water, heading straight for us.

"Why doesn't it turn, Mama?"

"The captains will surely take care of it," she replied, her voice quavering.

The *Empress* steamed forward again, gathering speed, but the other boat looked less than fifty yards away. A huge white "K" was painted on the single black funnel. Through a megaphone, a commanding voice hailed the oncoming freighter.

My knees shook. "It's going to hit us!" Mama pulled me away from the rail. I clutched a braid in each hand and gnawed the ends of both, my eyes glued to the approaching ship.

A long blast sounded across the ever-shrinking space between us and the other boat.

Ten yards.

Five.

We huddled low against the wall.

The deck jolted. Screaming, we fell down hard.

The grinding of metal ripped apart the calm night.

Sparks flew.

A crewman shouted, "We've been struck amidships!"

I regained my footing. Back at the rail, I shrieked in horror. The freighter was jammed into the middle of the *Empress* about forty yards away from me. Its hull reached as high as the deck below where I stood. My pulse raced. No one in the collision path could have survived. The screeching of steel against steel bombarded our ears.

"The collier's pulling away," yelled the man craning his neck through the porthole beneath me.

"Mama, what do we do?" Upright again, she stared at her knuckles, white from clutching her handbag. "Mama!" I shook her arm, but she was frozen in place. It was hard to breathe. My heart hammered my ribs.

Water thundered through the gaping hole, surging into the lower decks. *HSSSSS!* The noise came from below, as if water poured on the heated boulders of a giant's sauna. A vile smell stung my nostrils and made my stomach clench.

A siren pierced the air.

"All hands to the boats!" Crew members scurried to their lifeboat stations and set to work at a feverish pace.

"MAMA!"

She snapped out of her daze. "Jussi. I must get him. Take my handbag and get into a lifeboat."

"Don't leave me!"

But she was gone.

Terror gripped me.

What if she didn't return? The back of my head and neck tingled. Should I follow her? People charged out of the doorway where Mama had vanished. There were so many I'd never get past them.

The deck of the ship started to tilt, pressing my left hip and leg against the bars. I clung to the solid railing. Passengers swarmed around me. Most wore only night-clothes. All wore fear on their faces. On an upper deck people clambered into a lifeboat.

I remembered New Year's Eve. Lead sputtered in the water pail. Uncle Arvo was saying, "...boat... black spots..." The small black shapes enlarged before my eyes into a giant, sinister ship. *Oh, God, if only my family could be together again.*

Suspended over the water, the lifeboat dipped sharply at one end. I screamed. Everyone on board toppled into the river.

"Mama! John!" I hollered into the bedlam, tears streaming. "I can't leave without you."

I flinched at the crashes of furniture and dishes inside the ship, and the wails of those trapped below. My legs trembled, itching to run, but with nowhere to go.

Men scrambled past. Women cried out for lost chil-dren. Everyone shouted or prayed.

One man stopped praying when he reached me. "You need this more than I do," he said, removing his life-belt. "Take off your coat. It'll weigh you down." I did so, and wriggled Mama's handbag over my shoulder. He fastened the cork-filled canvas vest around me, tying the straps as tightly as they would go. The handbag pinched my armpit.

Before I could thank him, the gentleman climbed

over the rail and jumped. I whispered a prayer for his safety. His splash came a moment later.

I leaned against the starboard railing. It tipped farther over by the minute. How long before it would reach the river? Panic paralyzed my brain.

Deck chairs and pieces of equipment slid by me. Some were snagged by the railing, others fell into the water.

The main lights went out. A few lamps on one of the upper decks still shone. Despite the chill, sweat beaded on my forehead. Gooseflesh covered my arms.

Think, Saara, think. Papa would know what to do. Like when I was four and our house caught on fire. He had helped me climb out of my bedroom window and we'd jumped into the snowdrifts.

More people flung themselves into the black river. A lifeboat hung tangled in its lines while crewmen hacked at the ropes trying to set it free. Only a handful of boats had been launched—with little time to load passengers. The ship tilted drastically. Time was running out.

There was no sign of Mama on the crowded deck. A small figure stumbled beside the wall. He looked like my brother.

"JOHN! OVER HERE!"

John skidded toward me, his face ghostly in the low light. I caught hold of his lifebelt to keep him from slipping between the rails.

"I'm scared!" He grabbed my arms. "There were whistles... and a b-bump... you and Mama were gone." He looked around the angled deck. "Where's Mama?"

"She went to find you. She'll be back soon." He wailed.

I desperately hoped I was right. *God, keep her safe.*

Two decks above us a woman screamed, lost her grip on the railing, and careened into the water.

"The b-boat's tipping over! What do we do?" Shivering in his pyjamas and bare feet, John seemed tinier than ever. "I can't swim!"

Soon he'd be hysterical. In my best horse-steadying tone I said, "Calm down, John."

My insides turned somersaults. It was all like a horrible dream—like the very worst nightmare. If it were a dream, I would sprout wings and fly to shore... but it wasn't a dream, it was real, and we had to do whatever we could to save ourselves.

But how could I leave knowing that Mama was still inside the ship? She had told me to get into a lifeboat, yet the crew had given up trying to launch more boats. Instead they were pitching deck chairs and lifebuoys overboard. Soot rained down on us from the funnels.

John whimpered. I hugged him. Fighting to steady my voice, I said, "I'll keep you safe."

If we waited until the rail touched the river, we could get trapped underwater by the upper decks. As if Papa were speaking to me, I recalled what he'd said before leaping from our burning house. I repeated his words to my brother. "We have to jump before it's too late."

"I can't!"

"JOHN, LISTEN. We both have lifebelts." I tried hard to sound brave. "I'll help you. WE'LL JUMP TOGETHER."

"NO!"

A man's large hand grabbed my arm. "Not from here. Go forward!" He pointed toward the ship's bow, then at the mast. "Get clear of the rigging."

I looked up at the tall pole and collection of wires and gasped. Pulling John with me, we followed the man. Pushed on by others crowding us from behind, we groped our way. We stumbled and swayed, but somehow kept our footing.

When the man stepped over the rail and jumped, I stared down at the river. It frothed with swimmers and debris. My knees trembled. The water was closer to us than the snow had been to Papa and me, but still my head spun from the height.

A space appeared. Swallowing my fear, I breathed a quick prayer. "We have to go *now*—hold your breath."

I grasped John's hand and we leaped together.

When I hit the surface my lifebelt thrust upward and struck my chin. The shock of the icy water wrenched John's hand away as we went under. Skin instantly chilled. Every nerve in my body protested.

Holding my breath, I battled against panic. I tumbled every which way in the inky black water.

Choking terror.

Finally my throbbing head broke the surface. I gulped air. Coughed up salty river water. Lungs and nose in searing pain.

My left shoulder banged and scraped against splintered wood. People thrashed about, frantic to survive. Water plugged my ears, muffling their cries.

The *Empress* towered above, like a huge black cliff

bearing down on me.

I touched something clammy—a lifeless body, a bloody gash on her head. I screamed, my stomach lurched, I vomited.

"John!" I gurgled, spitting out water. "Where are you?"

Many voices moaned or wailed, but not my little brother's. The loudest voice of all roared in my head: Papa's. "I expect you to watch out for your brother."

I must find him. "God, help me."

CHAPTER

14

"John!"

Was he trapped underwater? I shoved a piece of wooden grating out of the way. Then a partly submerged suitcase. My chin stung when it brushed against the rough life-belt.

I reached down as far as possible fishing for John while keeping my face above water. My arms felt stiff and clumsy. If only there were more light. The remaining lamps on the *Empress* were faint in the mist.

How long could he hold his breath? Turning, my hands hunted. Metal. Canvas. My leg grazed something jagged.

He could be drowning. The thought turned my muscles weak.

I felt hair. Short hair. I grabbed a bunch and pulled. Stuck. He was pinned somehow. Tears sprang to my eyes. I strained at the hair again.

It wasn't John who bobbed to the surface. It was a man—dead. I gagged.

"Move away from the ship," gasped a swimmer as he passed me. "She'll suck you under."

I desperately wanted to get away. My fingers were going numb in the frigid water. Mama's handbag dug into my side. But to remove it I'd need to undo my lifebelt. That would be too dangerous.

The deck railing we'd climbed over moments before rapidly approached the water. How could this be happening? The *Empress,* that massive boat, would soon disappear.

"Help!" screamed a small lifebelted form thrashing the water between me and the ship. "Saara!"

"John!" I kicked madly toward him, panic gripping my throat. It was totally against my instincts to swim nearer to the *Empress,* but I had to reach my brother before he was crushed. Or caught in the wires!

My arms windmilled.

"Help!" John blubbered and coughed.

Almost there.

"Help me, Saara!"

Two more strokes.

His eyes wild with fright, he clutched at my head.

"Let go," I tried to shout, but it hurt to draw that much air into my lungs. I twisted out of his fumbling reach and grabbed him from behind, by the hair. He yelped. It was just long enough to clench in my fist, leaving one arm free to paddle.

"I c-c-can't... swim."

"Kick your legs."

He was shivering. His legs were sluggish. John wasn't

as close to the *Empress* as I had feared, but we had to get out of the way before she rolled on her side. Thank goodness John wore a lifebelt so he could float. I towed him away from the ship as quickly as I could, struggling to avoid his flailing arms.

We made progress, but would the gigantic ship roll too fast and hit us? The grinding metal sounded like death screams. Were we clear yet of where the wires would come down?

"Paddle with your arms, John. Yes! Pull the water."

My legs got snarled in my sodden dress. I tore at it and the skirt part came away completely. My boots were anchors, but there was no way to remove them.

Howls of agony pierced the foggy night.

"It's so d-d-dark," said John. "I c-can't tell where the b-boat is!"

I would not give up. I *could not* give up.

"John, kick!" He wriggled, but he couldn't move his legs anymore. My hands went numb. My eyes alone told me I still held onto my brother.

SLAP! I glanced back. The fog had cleared enough for us to see that the ship's funnels had hit the water. The mast and wires had missed us. We were safe.

Hordes of people clung to the hull crying, "HELP! HELP!"

I saw the white shape of a lifebelt around a person disappear into a funnel—sucked down like a drain! A force began to drag at us. I pulled hard at the water. Wreckage pounded my back.

Bodies popped to the surface like corks. Desperate

souls kicked and clawed, using anything to stay afloat—even corpses.

The *Empress* rumbled. An explosion blasted water into the air, spraying us. I blinked away the drops.

HSSSS! The ship plunged. Vanished. The river had swallowed her whole.

"Lights... g-g-gone," mumbled John.

Icy water sucked at our bodies. I fought against it, struggling to keep hold of my brother. Tightening my grip on his hair, I headed for the greenish glow of a life-buoy floating in the distance.

The crest of a monstrous wave swept us high. I gulped a breath and clutched John as it spun us round. Under. Rolling.

Burst through the surface. We gasped precious air, coughing and sputtering. John whimpered.

Oh, so weak. The temptation to relax in the frigid water was overpowering. There was no one to help us. Were we going to die? Would we never see Mama again? Or Papa?

A woman in an overcoat drifted in the current. Her arms twitched. She slumped face-down in the water. Her head didn't lift again. The corpse of a child floated next to her.

I sobbed. If only Papa were here to rescue us.

John's arms went limp.

"NO. I won't let you die!" Drawing him closer to me, I heard him moan and felt his tremors.

"Em... presh," he said, slurring the word. "Shaara."

I kicked to boost myself onto a floating table, but

slipped backwards. With a fierce grunt I hauled myself farther up, but the weight of my brother pulled me off the smooth wood.

"G-God, help us," I prayed, shivering. Cold stabbed me bone-deep.

I wrapped my arm around one table leg. My neck jerked sideways. Something, or someone, snagged one of my braids. I yelped. My head was being pulled under the water.

"Let go, woman," ordered a man's voice. "Are you insane?"

He freed my braid, then steered a deck chair toward the woman. "Here's your own raft."

The man seized me around the waist. "Up you go, lass." He shoved me onto the table. Together we heaved until John lay beside me.

I whispered, "Thank... you," while gripping my brother with the last shreds of my strength.

"Stay put. When I reach the rescue ship," he said, gesturing across the water, "I'll send help your way." The stranger—our angel—swam off with powerful strokes.

There in the distance shone the lights of a freighter. Between scraps of fog I saw a white "K" on the black funnel. It was the boat that had struck the *Empress*.

All about us in the river people clamoured to be rescued.

John and I huddled together. "Help is... c-c-coming," I told him.

His quivering stopped. Was he still breathing? I squeezed him tightly. "John... say something!"

No answer. I boxed his ear. Thank heavens he groaned.

There was no longer any feeling in my lower body. It was impossible to move my legs. Could I hang on long enough to be saved? I shivered violently, teeth chattering. I yearned to put my head down and go to sleep.

John coughed, still alive.

My eyelids drooped.

"Stay a... wake, Saara," I told myself, forcing my eyes wide open.

A lantern swung back and forth in the mist.

"O... ver... here," I called, raising my frozen hand. "Help... p-please."

A man in the lifeboat shouted, "Two children dead ahead."

"We're not... d-dead yet," I whispered.

My eyes closed, giving in to exhaustion. I could no longer feel the cold.

15

"Missy, wake up," said a male voice with a Norwegian accent. He sounded a mile away.

Someone jostled me. My arms were rubbed. I drifted back to the light, to ice-cold misery again. All I wanted was the blackness.

"Here, Missy, drink this," he said, louder. A cup pressed on my lips, and a cool, fiery liquid poured down my throat. I coughed, trying to spit it out. "Never had whiskey, yes?"

Feeling had returned to my fingers. I held a fistful of hair. John's hair.

I lay on a berth, pressed against somebody whose feet were near my face. A thin wool blanket scratched my neck. My lifebelt was gone. Mama's handbag lay tucked at my side. The only parts of me not frigid were my head and throat, which felt on fire.

Some time later, still dark, arms lifted me. I shivered and

was faintly aware of men's voices, saying, "…transfer to *Lady Evelyn*… dock at Rimouski."

Dawn broke. I lay on something hard. It was the deck of a boat. I saw a steam vent nearby. People huddled around it, barely clothed, some naked, their skin blue. Faces were blank and haggard. No brother, no mother, only strangers. I clung to Mama's drenched handbag, perhaps all I had left of her. I cried out for Mama, my voice hoarse. A stranger held me securely. She rocked me as I sank back into the beckoning darkness.

With my eyes closed I saw the *Empress of Ireland* floating peacefully in brilliant sunlit waters. A thunderhead brooded, looming on the horizon. Darkness fell. The entire ship transformed into molten lead covered with large black spots and sizzled to the river bottom.

A girl screamed. She sounded a lot like me. I thrashed about, ignoring my pain, clawing toward the surface of the water.

Someone's arms wrapped around me, and a voice said, "It's all right. You're safe now." She wore crisp white clothes and smelled like medicine.

"Better give her something to help her sleep," said a gruff voice. "I'll remove her dinner. She won't be eating for a while yet."

Mama passed John in the corridor of the *Empress*. He was hidden by the swarm of passengers rushing toward the open deck.

"Mama, turn around," I called.

She struggled to reach our cabin with the floor tilting.

"NO!" I screamed. "Get out! You'll be trapped."

"There, there," spoke a soothing female voice. She tucked a soft blanket around my shoulders. I blinked. My dream had been so realistic, yet I wasn't on a boat anymore. A friendly nurse stood beside my bed. The room didn't look like a hospital, more like a fancy hotel.

"Mama... John—where are they?"

"You must rest. In the morning, more will be known."

I tried to sleep, but soon I was covered in sweat. Waves of shivers swept over me, starting with my legs and ending with my jaw. I couldn't stop my teeth from tapping together. "P-papa, I n-need you."

In the throes of fever, I pictured Mama either stepping into a lifeboat unharmed or screaming as she drowned. I didn't know what was real. When I did wake up enough to feel the pain of my injuries, I was terrified to return to my nightmares.

I smelled the strong odour of antiseptic. A cold thermometer worked its way under my tongue. Who held my wrist? She had red hair under her nurse's cap.

Reading the temperature, she smiled, saying, "Much better. Your fever is starting to come down."

"Mama." I choked on fear. "I don't know... where... my brother..." Sobs shook me.

"Hush, now." The nurse offered me a handkerchief. I wiped my eyes and blew my nose. "What is your name, dear?"

"Saara."

She reached into the bedside cupboard and pulled out a mangled leather handbag. "Saara, is this your mother's?"

I nodded.

"Was your father on the ship as well?"

"No, he… if he was… maybe he could have saved her," I said, sorrow making each word a lead weight.

"She may still be alive, since you—"

"But she went back to our cabin…" It hurt too much to remember.

"In any case, the CPR will wire your father so he can fetch you. What is the city and what is his name?"

After I spelled Papa's name, she said, "Hmm… foreign-sounding name. Were you not in first class?"

"No, third class. Our name is Finnish."

She shook her head, saying, "'Tis a miracle you survived."

"My brother, John, is he here too?"

"Age?"

"Eight."

"No, not here at the Château Frontenac. I will ask at the hospital. Now you need to rest."

Wherever John was, I hoped he, too, had someone sending a telegram to Papa.

Darts of morning sunlight stabbed my eyes as the curtains were flung open. Squinting, I recognized the red-haired nurse.

"Have you found my brother?"

"I'm terribly sorry, dear. There are no boys listed at the hospital."

"Where is he?" Curling my hands into fists shot painful spasms up my arms. I winced and rubbed my left shoulder.

"When your father arrives he will investigate. There is much uncertainty still."

Perhaps John had been too cold for too long. *Hurry, Papa.*

16

When the nurse returned to check my temperature, I said, "My brother was with me when I was rescued. Please help me find him."

"Dreams can be mighty persuasive, dear. Now open your mouth."

"What day is it?" I managed to blurt before she jammed the thermometer under my tongue.

She straightened the covers around me. "You arrived Friday evening, and it's now Sunday afternoon, the thirty-first of May."

Wide-eyed, I gagged, almost swallowing the thermometer. She whisked it out, asking, "What's the matter?"

"Today is my birthday." Ragged sobs overtook me.

"Oh, Saara." She held me, stroking my matted hair, twined in the braids Mama had made on Thursday morning. One plait still had its blue ribbon that she'd tied near the tip.

"If my mother survived, wouldn't she have found me by now?"

"There were hundreds rescued from the *Empress*, dear, many of them foreigners with next to no English."

"Like Mama," I said under my breath.

"When your father arrives, he will speak to the authorities."

I couldn't wait to see Papa. He would be so happy to find me alive. Church bells rang in the distance.

"Saara, you need to get to the lavatory. We'll go slowly. Lean on my arm as much as necessary," she said, pulling back the covers and helping me sit up.

Either my eyes or the room spun around, I couldn't tell. Below my nightgown were spindly legs, scraped and covered with purple bruises. As I attempted to stand, they trembled, but held me up. At a turtle's pace I wobbled forward, grateful for the nurse's support.

Later, back in bed, my stomach rumbled. When my lunch appeared, I gobbled every drop of soup and crumb of bread. I'd slept so much in the past couple of days that I lay awake for ages. I regretted that John wasn't with me in the "castle," as he'd called the Château Frontenac the day we left on the ship. He would have been thrilled.

Restless, I eased onto my side, leaned over, and opened the bedside cupboard. Inside was a cloth bundle. Undoing the knotted kerchief, I found a simple old-fashioned white dress and my own new boots, dull and warped.

I spotted Mama's handbag. Opening the clasp, I took out the water-stained case that held the silver spoon. My breath caught in my throat. The spoon would not reach my aunt in Finland. I would not meet my grandparents.

154

Mama was gone.

My last glimpse of her—rushing to find John—flashed into my head. *Don't leave me.*

The thought of being without her for the rest of my life wrenched my stomach. My heart ached more than my battered body. Much more. I felt completely alone. That image from the boat stuck, no matter how hard I tried to picture something, anything, else. I cried and cried until my tears ran out.

Monday morning brought a short, gruff nurse to my bedside. Her black hair was drawn so tightly into a bun it must have made her head hurt. "Your nightgown is lovely, but it's time you were properly dressed."

"It isn't mine."

"Likely a gift from a generous soul in Rimouski, along with this," she said, stooping to pick up the dress from the cupboard. Yes, I remembered hearing a kind woman speaking to me in sing-song French. She had fed me salty broth and I felt safe.

I struggled to sit up. My stiff arms felt heavy as I lifted the clothing over my head. The pressure from the left sleeve made me wince. The nurse buttoned my dress and laced my boots in no time. She unravelled my braids, forcing a brush through my tangled hair. Sorrow washed over me. That was Mama's job.

"Don't braid it."

"Leaving hair of this length down will not do." Her hands were swift and rough, smelling of iodine. I missed Mama's touch.

When she was done, I leaned on her arm and stood on my tender legs—yes, they were steady.

"For a change of scenery you can eat your breakfast at the end of the hallway." She carried my covered plate while escorting me to a small table by the window. I walked like Fred's grandmother with her crippled joints.

We passed a man with a stitched gash on his cheek. The nurse's greeting didn't alter his vacant stare or his silence. She whispered, "Lost his wife of twenty-some years." What little strength I had drained away.

At the table, the nurse uncovered my serving of fried eggs and toast, and left. What caught my eye wasn't the view outside, but a newspaper with the one-inch headline *"910 LIVES WERE LOST AND 477 SAVED."* Phrases leaped out of the printed columns. "Empress *sank in less than fifteen minutes," "gruesome harvest of the dead," "very few women saved,"* and *"launched into eternity."*

The smell of grease made me gag. I retreated to my room as quickly as my stiff muscles would allow. Burying my face in the pillow muffled my cries. Mama was dead. It was my fault. I could run faster so I should have gone to the cabin for John. If I hadn't been sick, the three of us would have been together... asleep... trapped. It was too horrible to imagine.

After lunch on Tuesday I paced the hotel corridor, grimacing each time I forced my legs to take bigger steps. Clusters of men recounted how they'd survived the tragedy.

A lady with one arm in a sling described her reunion

with her husband on the rescue train from Rimouski to Quebec. "I was so utterly convinced he'd drowned that when I first saw him I swore he was a ghost."

Nurse "Gruff" found me at the far end. "You have a visitor. He's in your room."

Papa.

Clenching my jaw against the pain, I hurried to find Papa.

When I saw his familiar tall frame, shyness overtook me. He stood facing the window, mumbling in Finnish. Once I'd crept close enough to hear his words, they stopped me in my tracks.

"I should have gone with you, Emilia... I could have helped you get Jussi out." He slumped, face in his hands. "Jussi..."

Could he think of no one else but John?

Papa shook his head. "You were afraid of the boat. Why did I let you go? My son..."

Welling tears prickled my eyes.

Papa groaned. "You needed me and I wasn't there."

My nose ran, so I sniffed.

He whipped around.

Trembling, I looked into his dark-rimmed red eyes. His face was haggard. Although he stared at me, his expression remained blank.

He didn't care about me. I felt my hope slip from my grasp like a china ornament, falling, smashing to the floor.

I turned away.

Something grazed the back of my head. Papa's hand? "Saara."

He motioned for me to sit on the bed and pulled the chair over for himself. His mouth twitched. "Were you hurt badly?"

"Some bruises, scrapes… I'm sore and tired, but fine."

"I believed all of you were lost until your telegram reached me." His intense blue eyes bore into mine. "Facing life without Mama and Jussi…" He paused, his voice choked with emotion.

Life without Mama. I took fast, shallow breaths.

He continued, "It made me realize how precious…" A teardrop trickled as far as his moustache and disappeared. "What happened to them?"

I flinched, reminded of the disaster. "Didn't you receive a telegram about John?"

"No, I've heard nothing." He held out his hands, palms up. "Their names aren't on the list of survivors, and I couldn't find their bodies at the dockside morgue." He drew in a big breath. "I was told only a few children were rescued, all girls. Your mother and Jussi, they must be dead—"

"You're wrong!" I shouted.

Papa's eyes widened at my outburst.

"I watched out for John like you told me to do." My whole body quivered. I had never in my life spoken like that to him.

My tongue felt swollen, as if to dam my words. I gulped. "John and I were on the deck and jumped into the river together."

"Where was Mama?"

Focusing on my lap, I relived that dark night on the ship, scene by scene, like a play. No matter how painful it was, I forced myself to tell him everything I could remember.

"I didn't see Mama again after she left me at the railing, but John was with me in the water." My confidence grew as the image of him beside me on the floating table sharpened in my mind.

"Was Jussi alive?"

"He was coughing when the rescuers saw us." There was a hazy memory of being gripped under my arms, and being dragged over the hard edge of the lifeboat. "I... I don't remember what happened to John after that. I've asked the nurses to help me find him, but they told me to wait for you to come."

My father said nothing for a long time. He bent over and drooped his head.

If John had died, surely his body would have been in the morgue. *Oh, God, if John is alive, please help us find him.*

Papa cradled his face in his hands. "Where is my son?"

Suppose it *was* a dream? But I couldn't have imagined it, could I? No, I had held John's hair in my fist.

"Papa, I remember more! A man said, 'Let go now, Miss, we've got him.' I was clenching John's hair. They pried open my fingers. He *was* rescued. We have to find him!"

I jumped to my feet, making myself light-headed. In the hallway, I stopped a nurse I hadn't seen before. "You must help us. My brother was rescued but we don't know where he is." I gave his name and age.

She tapped her chin with an index finger. "Hmm... some passengers are being lodged on the steamer *Alsatian*... but first I will telephone all of the hospitals."

"Yes, please," I said, as she left. Papa stood in the doorway of my room looking dazed.

The nurse returned after several minutes. "There *is* a young boy in the Detention Hospital. The staff think he's six or seven. He's extremely ill with congestion of the lungs."

"He could be John!" His lungs had been weakened by pneumonia, and I knew he had swallowed a lot of water. "Papa, we have to go there."

"Shall I request a taxi?" said the nurse. Papa agreed.

For years I had imagined that my first drive in an automobile would be fast and exciting, not the quiet, tense ride it turned out to be. Each time a wheel dipped into a hole or hit a bump I cringed and my shoulder throbbed.

Once we located the correct ward, we were shown to the boy's room. Our steps quickened. Hope swelled. A shiver crept along my back.

There he lay, curled up on his side, eyes closed.

My heart leaped at the sight of his hair—light brown, like my brother's. I gasped. It was missing a patch on top.

"John!"

"Jussi!"

161

His eyelids fluttered. "Pa… pa."

Papa knelt by the bed and enveloped John's small hand in his own. "My son, my son."

I wept freely. "Thank you, dear God."

"Mama?" John said, followed by a barking cough. His face was scratched and bruised.

"Jussi, don't worry about Mama. You need to concentrate on getting better."

John's eyes shut.

We watched him sleep. Papa didn't let go of John's hand for a full hour.

Eventually Papa said, "We'll come back tomorrow, Jussi. Sleep well."

"Goodbye, John," I whispered, and kissed his cheek.

In silence, Papa and I ate our supper of roasted chicken and crusty white bread in a tiny restaurant on a cobblestone street.

After the waiter removed the dishes, Papa cleared his throat. "When I first arrived in your hotel room, I was in a fog of grief. Then you appeared, white-faced and frail." He gazed at the flickering candle on the table. "My mind tricked me into seeing you in a coffin." Papa leaned forward, his eyes intent on me. "But you were alive. I felt more blessed than I did at your birth."

Unable to speak, I simply nodded and smiled.

We strolled back to the Château Frontenac. Although Papa was overjoyed at finding John, his eyes held sadness. Like a dark cloud above our heads was the question of what had happened to Mama.

18

"Saara," a weak voice called.

I woke in a sweat, the room black, my heart beating wildly. It wasn't the same nightmare I'd had over and over since the boat sank. Instead, I saw a misty shoreline and heard Mama's voice. Whenever I drifted back to sleep, the plaintive call came again. Since the dream refused to stop, I decided to stay awake.

How would we cope without Mama... her cooking... her sewing... her defending me? How would Papa treat me once we returned home? I dreaded going back to Port Arthur. Papa showed no pride in me for saving John. But it didn't matter. I knew I had done what was right. I had never given up. A flame of joy glowed inside me that no one could blow out. I was determined to do everything I could to care for my brother.

Long before breakfast I was washed and dressed, anxious for Papa to arrive so we could see John again. At the hospital we found him asleep. After watching him breathe for ten minutes, Papa suggested we get some coffee. Near the stairwell we heard someone running after us.

"Mr. Mäki," said the nurse, "do you speak Finnish?" Papa nodded. "There's a survivor at the Jeffrey Hale Hospital, a woman, who is frantic and cannot speak English. Will you go to translate for her, please?"

"Yes, of course. When my son wakes up, tell him we will return as soon as possible."

"Certainly, Mr. Mäki. I'll call for a taxi."

"She could be Mama!" If my legs hadn't hurt so much, I would have skipped on our way back to the street.

At the Jeffrey Hale Hospital, the nurse-in-charge met us in the lobby. "She's becoming hysterical. This way, please."

Before we stepped into the woman's room, I knew she wasn't Mama. She sounded so young, screaming for her baby. My heart sank through the floor and I wanted to scream, too. How foolish of me to think she could have been my mother.

As soon as the distraught woman heard Papa speaking Finnish, she grabbed his arm and poured out her story. She had travelled from Minneapolis, Minnesota, with her six-month-old son. In the river, she lost her grip on her baby. "They must find him."

Papa strove to interpret and to calm her, but she began to wail again. I couldn't stand it and slipped out of the room, crying until my head hurt.

The nurse-in-charge thanked Papa for his help.

"You're welcome. I must ask you, is there an Emilia Mäki in this hospital?" He gave the spelling.

She checked the records. "I'm sorry. There is no patient by that name."

We trudged along the corridor.

A faint voice said a word that sounded like "Saara."

"I think I heard someone calling my name."

Papa stopped and listened with me for a few moments. I strained my ears, but did not hear it again.

"It must have been your imagination," he said. "Let's get back to Jussi." Papa headed for the exit.

"Wait. What if Mama *is* here and she's hurt so badly she can't tell them her name?"

His eyebrows met as he considered my idea.

"I have her handbag, so they wouldn't know who she is."

"We could ask."

Papa approached a nurse busy filling in a chart. "Pardon me." She glanced up, tucking a loose strand of black hair behind her ear. "Do you have any unidentified patients from the *Empress*? Perhaps a Finnish woman?"

"Finnish I can't say, but she's certainly a foreigner. She's hardly spoken a word, much less French or English. Follow me."

We entered a room with four beds. She pointed to one by the window. There lay a thin, pale woman with closed eyes, one severely swollen with a huge black welt below it. Her head was swathed in bandages. There was nothing familiar about her. I blinked away tears.

"Are you satisfied now?" said Papa, turning on his heel and leaving the room.

I blindly headed toward the door.

"Jussi."

The softly spoken word came from the bed by the window. I stared at the bandaged "foreigner."

"Saara," she whispered.

"Sawra." The sound was like beautiful music. With a surge of energy, I ran to her side and grasped her hand. "I'm here, Mama. It's Saara."

Her eyes opened, glassy and dull. They flickered with recognition. She inhaled sharply as her arm encircled me. "Thanks be to God."

From the hall came the sound of my father's heavy footsteps.

I called out, "Mama's alive!"

Papa stood in the doorway, dumbstruck.

He sped to Mama's side. "Emilia? I... I thought you were gone forever." He embraced her while she repeated his name. When he pulled away, he studied her bandages. "Your head—does it hurt much?"

"Nothing compared to here," she said, tapping her chest, "grieving the loss of our children." She stroked Papa's unshaven cheek. "I prayed that Saara would survive, but Jussi..." Her eyes overflowed. "I never reached him. Tauno, I tried so hard... people pushed me, screaming—" Mama's sobs shook her whole body, making her wince and touch her forehead.

"Mama," I said, "John found his way to the deck. He was rescued, too."

Mama's eyes flashed between Papa's face and mine. She cried out in astonishment. More tears flowed. "God is gracious indeed."

166

Later, a petite nurse entered the room carrying a tray of dressing supplies. "*Bonjour*, are you her family?"

"Yes, I am her husband, and this is our daughter."

"*Très bien.*"

"And my little brother is in another hospital."

"Were all of you on the *Empress*?"

"No, only Mama, John, and me."

"When Madame finally became conscious she wept and said 'yoosy' and 'sawra' over and over. It broke my heart. Now I'm so happy for her." She set down her tray. "I apologize, but I must change her bandages."

Papa smiled and reached for Mama's hand. "We'll go and wake up Jussi to tell him the good news."

CHAPTER

19

I rolled over in my own bed and heard the murmur of conversation from downstairs. Sipu purred beside me. She offered her silky coat for me to stroke. When I had wakened in the dark earlier, heart thumping, I thought I would never get back to sleep.

Sitting up, I looked around my bedroom as if I were a stranger. There were my "treasures"—the robin's nest, the piece of amethyst rubbed smooth, and the horse-shoes. I smiled. What had been so precious to me two weeks before now seemed unimportant.

On the dresser sat the lead boat from New Year's Eve. Errors in the fog of the St. Lawrence had stolen my predicted voyage: dream exchanged for nightmare. A wave of gooseflesh covered my arms. I hastily buried the tiny boat under my winter stockings in the bottom drawer.

Judging by the bright sky, I was surely late for school. I threw on my dress and bolted down the stairs.

My parents were sipping coffee at the kitchen table, the

dirty breakfast dishes pushed aside. Papa held Mama's hand.

"What time is it?" I asked.

Papa looked up. "You had better hurry. It's almost nine o'clock."

"No one woke me up. I—"

"Tauno, you tease," said Mama. "Saara, you don't have to go to school."

"I don't?" I'd forgotten what teasing from Papa felt like.

"I need your help around here today." Mama re-arranged the small pillow on the chair that supported her ankle, which was encased in a plaster cast. Early purple lilacs, crowded into a quart sealer, filled the air with their sweet scent. Papa scooped porridge into a bowl and set it at my spot. I grimaced at the lumpy cereal.

"Papa did a fine job being the cook this morning." Mama beamed her appreciation his way. "After you eat, Saara, I need you to run down to the Co-op for a pound of coffee and—"

"Emilia, stop fussing about food," said Papa, stacking the cups and saucers. "The church ladies are bringing meals for us."

Papa had agreed to that? A glob of oats stuck in my throat. Thank goodness he wouldn't be trying to cook supper.

He placed the dishes in the sink and sighed. "Did you notice how long the employment lines were yesterday? If I don't get going, all the jobs will be snatched up. I have to find steady work soon."

There wasn't even a sliver of hope in his voice.

"Tauno, now you need to stop fretting. God will provide." Mama smiled up at him. "We needed you in Quebec, and the church's collection more than paid your fare. We won't starve."

"Food is one thing, but we have rent to pay and I will not accept charity for that." With his mouth set in a hard, bitter line, he hastened out of the house.

"Papa hasn't changed at all."

"Oh, Saara, you're wrong. But his worries are great."

She slowly spun her wedding ring.

"Before you came downstairs he was telling me about the morgue in Quebec. He searched row after row after row of coffins looking for Jussi and me." Her voice cracked. She brushed tears from her cheeks. "Give him time."

I forced myself to eat the rest of my porridge and drank an extra glass of milk to clear the lumps. "Where's John?"

"Still sleeping."

"Should I check on him?"

"How about after the dishes are washed? If you bring me a tea towel I can dry—"

"It's all right, Mama. I can do both."

"Bless you."

I busied myself at the sink. Mama said, "I am so grateful to be home. Though I wish I could do more." She sighed. "Could you fetch my knitting basket, please? Perhaps there is enough leftover wool for a baby sweater."

To the sound of her clicking needles, I cleaned up the kitchen. Afterwards, when I headed for the steps, Mama said, "I want Jussi down here so I can keep my eye on him. He can rest in the parlour."

Upstairs I had to jostle him awake and hold his arm to walk as he felt so weak still. "I can read to you, if you like."

"Okay."

With John and Mama settled in the parlour, I began reading. His eyelids drooped, but he smiled at a funny part.

Rap-rap-rap-rap. Whoever was knocking was determined to be heard. I laid down the book and rushed to open the front door. The stranger in a suit said, "Good morning, Miss. Is this the Mäki residence?"

"Yes, sir."

"You must be the famous Saara."

"Saara, yes. Famous, no."

"Definitely modest." He held forth his right hand. "Harry Taylor, *Daily News.* I'd like to hear how you and your family escaped the *Empress of Ireland*, if I may."

"Come in." I led him into the parlour and explained to Mama why he was there. He removed his bowler hat and they shook hands.

With pencil poised over his notebook, Mr. Taylor said, "Saara, please describe what happened."

"My mother and I were on the open deck because I felt sick. My brother was asleep in our cabin. The freighter was a few miles away when I first saw its lights." I didn't know a pencil could fly across the page with such speed. It was necessary, however, to match the pace at which I told my story. The faster I recounted the events, the less likely I was to cry.

John sat by Mama, subdued. When Mr. Taylor asked him what he remembered, he refused to speak. Then it was Mama's turn. I translated sentence by sentence as she shared her experience.

"After the coal ship struck the *Empress*, I ran back inside to get my son. At the bottom of the stairs people jammed the corridor like logs in a river. I struggled toward our cabin."

I felt her panic as I spoke for her. "I was terrified and stumbled."

We'd come so close to losing Mama. I swallowed hard and kept translating her words. "The floor tilted more every second."

Mama paused, weeping. I clasped her hand. We each took a large breath. "The crowd forced me backwards. Somehow I reached the deck along the slanted stairs… so difficult to stand… I slid toward the railing… dropped into the freezing water… I remember nothing more until I woke up in the hospital with a raging headache."

Mr. Taylor stopped writing. "Your mother's survival is a mystery, but it's evident someone saved her life, too." He glanced at John, curled up in a ball, his head on Mama's lap. "What a story."

The next day, the *Daily News* printed our year-old family portrait on the front page, with the headline, "*ALL BUT FATHER WERE ON WRECKED EMPRESS*." From the kitchen I heard Papa's reaction when Mama showed him the newspaper in the parlour.

"That man *would* have to point out that I was not

along. I punish myself enough already for letting you go without me."

Mrs. Pekkonen brought over fish stew, *pulla*, and several back issues of the *Daily News*. A Port Arthur man and his ten-year-old son had not survived the disaster. Rescued was a woman from Fort William, but not her husband or eight-year-old son. That could have been John. Our escape was miraculous. Why us and not those others? It was too big a question for me to sort out.

The following morning I stepped outside, my stomach tangled. Why did I feel so anxious about returning to school? Nothing Senja would say or do could be worse than what I'd faced with the *Empress*.

I straightened and marched down the back lane, startling sparrows from the bushes. A door slammed. The Pekkonens' boarding house came into view, with Helena descending the stairs. She gazed in my direction and froze.

Would she walk with me? Or wave to me? Smile?

Nothing.

I hurried past her house, waiting until Secord Street to brush away my silly tears. Why had I imagined she'd want to be with me?

Richard emerged from his house when I reached his gate. "Hey, Miss Mäki."

I braced for his taunts.

"How's the... ah..." It wasn't like him to fumble for words. He shoved both hands into his pockets and studied his boots. "You did a bully job saving little Johnny."

I stared at my old "enemy" while my face grew hot. "Thank you."

"Well, I... I forgot something in the house. See you at school," he said, as he ran back up the steps.

June 10, 1914: the first time in history Richard said something pleasant to me. Had Helena heard him? Doubtful, as she was more than half a block away.

Mr. McKee had the class give me a hero's welcome, including a standing ovation. He requested I tell the entire story, even though he'd pinned the newspaper article to the wall.

At recess, the Senior Third girls surrounded me, except for Senja and someone with dark blond hair—I assumed Helena—who stood by the fence at the far side of the playground.

"You were *so* brave, Saara," gushed Doris.

"Well, I—"

"It must have been utterly horrifying to see the dead bodies."

"Sickening, yes, and—" Everyone congratulated me at once.

Then I spotted Helena. She was not at the fence, but hovered at the edge of the crowd. Why did she look odd? Oh! She had bangs! Then who was that girl with Senja? Before I could investigate, Doris herded her gaggle of girls, with me centre stage, back into the school.

When we were seated at our desks, Mr. McKee said, "During recess, the principal informed me of the following announcement from the school board: *In an effort to eradicate scarlet fever and measles, it has been decided that all public schools will be closed today at noon—"*

A number of boys whistled their approval. Helena still sat next to Senja, but Senja turned away to exchange wide grins with Edith.

"Furthermore, the schools will be closed for the remainder of the term."

The room erupted with cheers as loud as we dared.

"Therefore, in the short time we have left, students shall empty their desks and clean the blackboards."

How I had looked forward to my trip and to missing the last month of school. In the past few days I'd begun to dread returning to class. Instantly we'd been granted extended summer holidays. Life certainly brought unexpected changes.

Senja whisked her books out of her desk, dashed to Edith's side, and together they left the classroom. I cleaned out my desk and walked into the hall, where I found Helena waiting by the stairs.

"Hello, Saara."

It took a moment for me to speak. "Hello."

"I understand if you don't want to talk to me. But… I…" Her face paled. "What a horrendous time you've had. I read every single word in the newspaper."

"I couldn't believe they printed all the details," I said. I couldn't believe we were talking to each other, either.

"If you or John or your mother had been lost, I would have never forgiven myself for telling you to go on the *Empress of Ireland.* I missed you, Saara."

"You did? I thought you'd be too busy with Senja to notice I was gone." I failed to keep the hurt out of my voice.

Helena winced. "I don't blame you. But by the Saturday after you left, Senja wouldn't even look at me."

"Like you treated me at the restaurant."

"Saara... I..." she stammered, as the last of the freed students jostled by us. "I shouldn't have let Senja change how I behaved toward you. I was cruel and I'm sorry. Really, I am." Her eyes shone, hinting at tears.

Stunned, I said nothing.

Helena sagged and headed toward the stairs.

As painful as her choosing Senja over me had been, I longed for us to be friends again. "Helena, wait."

She paused. I reached out and squeezed her hand. "What happened after I left?"

"Senja's father got a job and they moved into their own rented house, right next door to Eeee-dith's," she said, pointing her nose in the air. "By the next day they were best friends."

"I can see them getting along."

"You know how they treated me," she said, pretending to squash an insect. "And look at this haircut Senja talked me into. I hate it."

It did look strange and made her face seem as round as a pie.

"You were right about Senja," said Helena. "She's nothing but trouble. The only reason she wanted me for a friend was that I did everything she told me to do—not like you."

Helena ducked her eyes. "Do you..." She looked at me. "Do you want to walk home together?"

I nodded. Helena linked her arm in mine.

20

The June 15 headline of the *Daily News* read, *"WAR IN EUROPE INEVITABLE."* Uneasiness filled the shops, the Big Finn Hall, the church. Even the sky added to the tension. Vivid ribbons of light flashed against black clouds over the bay while thunder growled and roared in the most dramatic thunderstorm old-timers could recall.

At home, John peppered Papa with questions. "If Canada joins the war, will you be a soldier?" he asked, with too much enthusiasm for my liking.

"Only those men who volunteer have to go to war, son. Perhaps there will be no need."

My throat tightened. "I hope you're right."

The following afternoon, Helena and I sat on the grass in her backyard. Leaning against the fence, we enjoyed the birch tree's cool shade.

"My father's arm is finally healed," said Helena. "He can work again, but he says he will sign up if Canada calls for soldiers." She pointed to her ankle. We stared at the ant marching toward her knee. Prodding it with blades of grass did nothing to alter its course. "I don't want my father to go, even though he says he'd be home by Christmas. It's hard enough having him away at the logging camp." Helena whisked the ant away with her hand.

"Before we left on our trip," I said, "my father was so difficult I couldn't wait to escape. He hasn't changed much, but I wouldn't want him to leave."

Helena tore up bunches of grass and flung the loose blades at the white tree trunk. The humidity increased. We were on the brink of war, the future more uncertain than ever, yet I felt secure.

"Why are you smiling?" said Helena.

"If we had reached Finland, right now I'd be half a world away full of anger toward my father."

"Are you saying that the *Empress* disaster was a good thing?"

"No, not that. Only that something good came out of it."

After a thoughtful silence, Helena stood and brushed off her light cotton dress. "I have to help serve coffee. The pastor's wife is coming. Perhaps I'll surprise my mother and go in before she calls for me."

"Careful, she might faint from astonishment." I giggled as Helena playfully bumped me shoulder to shoulder.

We said goodbye and I hiked up the lane to join my family at the kitchen table. I stirred sugar into my milky coffee. The night before I had turned my partly used scribbler into a journal, but I had only a stub of a pencil to write with. "Mama, I need to buy a new pencil."

Papa erupted. "We have no money for anything but rent." He scowled, his eyes an icy blue. "I refuse to move us in with Arvo so that you can write in your scribbler."

I was trying to "give him time" as Mama had asked, but I was ready to move in with Auntie and Uncle myself. What a relief that I heard a knock on the door and could excuse myself. There stood the letter carrier in his smart uniform and cap, mailbag slung crosswise. He handed me an envelope. "Would this belong to you, Miss?"

It was addressed to "Miss Sarah Mackie" with no house number, only "Foley Street." The envelope had a return address in Toronto. "Yes, I think so. Thank you."

Unfolding the letter in the parlour, I scanned to the bottom of the second page, to see whom it was from. Mr. Blackwell.

A flood of memories scrolled before me: the photograph at the ship's rail, Emmy the cat, playing with my chum Lucy-Jane in the sandpit, and our meal on the *Empress*. As those images spiralled down a black whirlpool, my skin crawled. I returned to the beginning of the letter:

Dear Miss Sarah,

It is my hope that this letter will find its way into your hands. I know that you survived the hideous disaster, for I saw you being carried off the rescue vessel at Rimouski. I have been praying for your recovery. I have dared to hope that your dear mother and brother also were spared. If not, please accept my heartfelt condolences.

I regret that I am unable to send you a photograph. My

camera was, of course, lost along with everyone's baggage.

Naturally, like my journal and Mr. McKee's books.

It is with immense sadness

I gulped, my heart beating rapidly.

that I tell you

"No, don't tell me," I whispered. I wanted to stop reading, but my eyes were drawn to the next words.

that we have lost our darling Lucy-Jane.

"NO!" A searing pain stabbed my heart. Gone was the numbness that had kept me from feeling grief over the loss of a thousand lives in the wreck.

"Saara, what is it?" called Mama from the kitchen.

Papa asked, "Are you hurt?"

Clutching the letter, I ran to Mama, tears streaming. In her arms, I struggled to speak. "It's... it's Lucy-Jane... she didn't survive." Mama crooned as she rocked me, stroking my head.

Papa gently released the crumpled papers from my fist. "May I read the letter aloud?" I nodded. At the mention of Lucy-Jane's name, Papa's voice trembled.

In the confusion and terror of the sinking we became separated, never to see her face again.

Lucy-Jane's jolly face flashed before me, her dark curls bouncing as she delighted in a joke. Her mouth contorted in a scream as the river snatched her away from her father and dragged her down. An icy chill gripped my back. Papa's eyes, full of compassion, swept over us.

From a wee lass her heart was full of love for Jesus, so I am confident that she is far happier now in His presence than ever in her earthly life.

Do I write this only to share our grief? No, for I believe there is a reason for all things. Sarah, your life has been spared for a purpose. Our Commissioner said, "Nothing happens by chance in this life. All the circumstances of our lives are directed by our wise and loving Heavenly Father."

May you know the blessing of the Lord's peace now and for the rest of your life.

Affectionately,
Mr. Blackwell

"The LORD thy God in the midst of thee is mighty; he will save, he will rejoice over thee with joy; he will rest in his love, he will joy over thee with singing." Zephaniah 3:17

"This man's words are true..." Papa's voice faltered. "There *is* a reason why you are here... all of you... and not..." He collapsed on a chair and slumped forward, arms and head resting on the table. He broke down in crushing sobs. To see my father cry like that made my agony a hundred times worse. I stood so that Mama could shuffle her chair alongside him. She reached her arm around his heaving shoulders.

We were speechless, absorbed in our thoughts. Mr. Blackwell believed that nothing happened by chance. Why was I still alive and not Lucy-Jane?

Papa became quiet. As John clomped downstairs, Papa pulled a handkerchief out of his trousers pocket and blew his nose.

Composed, he said, "Saara, if it had not been for you, Jussi would not be with us today." The hard edges of his face melted. "You have always been stubborn, but it took strength of character to save your brother's life. We Finns call that *sisu*. Thank you, daughter."

He stood, beckoning me to himself. I expected a pat on the head, but instead, he wrapped his arms around me. My face pressed against his solid chest. His ironed-imperfectly-by-me white shirt smelled of laundry soap. I could hardly believe his embrace and approval were real.

Papa held me at arm's length, his large hands cupping my shoulders. "You have lost a friend, but I know you are brave."

After supper I tidied the kitchen. Mama and Papa remained at the table, silent, while John played solitaire. Dishes washed, I swept the floor.

"The news about Lucy-Jane is tragic," said Papa. "I can imagine her parents' sorrow." He sighed. "But the fact that my family survived is reason for a celebration."

"I agree, Tauno," said Mama. "Could we wait until after Marja's baby comes and they are able to travel here?

By that time my ankle should be well healed."

"Jussi will be more himself, too." Papa tousled John's hair. "I believe someone's birthday was forgotten in all of this. Am I right, Saara-*kulta*?"

Saara-gold.

Despite my grief over Lucy-Jane, hearing my special name sent a thrill clear through me.

CHAPTER

21

At last it was time to celebrate my birthday, and our surviving the *Empress* disaster, and the birth of my cousin. Good news had come from Finland, too. My grandmother was gradually improving. Perhaps I would meet her someday after all.

We sat around the parlour eating dessert. The afternoon sun illuminated the wallpaper's tiny flowers and touched the faces of family and friends. Baby Sanni blissfully slept in Auntie's arms. I was so stuffed with good feelings I had no room for cake.

Helena stood. "Saara, since your journal was lost, I want you to have this." She held out a duplicate of the one she'd given me for the trip.

"I can't... it cost so much... Mama?"

"Never refuse a gift from one who loves you, Saara," whispered Mama.

"Thank you, Helena." I gave her a hug. Opening the brown leather cover, I read, *To Saara, Best Wishes, Helena,* the exact words she'd written before. Why had I expected anything else? Composition was Helena's worst subject. I looked at her flushed, expectant face and smiled.

Papa nudged John. "Go on, Jussi. You tell her."

My brother mumbled something about a new knife, then thrust a Coca-Cola coin purse at me. "Happy birthday." He dropped to the floor by Papa's feet, hiding his red cheeks.

"Mr. Ruohonen gave your brother a replacement pocket knife, so Jussi asked him for a novelty to give to you."

"Thank you, John." Feeling a lump inside the purse, I took a peek. Coca-Cola chewing gum!

Mama set down her cup and saucer on the embroidered cloth covering the parlour table. She rose to her feet, favouring her weak ankle, and withdrew a familiar brown leather case from her pocket. Tied around the water-stained case was my old hair ribbon, the one that had stayed attached to my braid after the *Empress* sank. I couldn't believe Mama had saved it. She untied the ribbon, opened the lid, and held up the silver sugar spoon.

"Marja requested that we present you with this," she said, placing the spoon in my hand, "in honour of your birthday, and more importantly, because you deserve to have it."

I blinked the mistiness away. *Never refuse a gift...*

With a tremor in her voice, Mama said, "May it remind you, your whole life long, of how much we all love you."

Our guests stayed until early evening. I helped tidy the parlour and wash the dishes before heading upstairs to my bedroom. Writing in my new journal could wait until morning, but I picked up my spoon for a closer look. As I crawled under the covers there was a knock on my door.

"Come in."

"You're still awake?" Papa settled himself on the edge of my bed and stared at the floor. "I came to tell you..." He paused and cleared his throat. "The way I've..." His eyes met mine. They were full of meaning. Was it regret? An apology? Memories poked up, scrambled together with the hurts I'd been hanging onto. They were too much a part of me to throw off yet. I pushed them back down.

There was something I needed to tell him. "I'm sorry for not saying goodbye when I left Port Arthur."

Sadness flitted across his face. He nodded and said, "You had reason. It..." He looked away and rubbed his hands together as if they were chilled. "I knew..." He coughed. "Now my little girl is twelve," he said, shaking his head. "Maybe you're too old, but..." He began to sing, "*Minä pikku tytölleni...*"

Tears spilled down my cheeks. I pulled up the sheet to wipe them away.

"Saara, what's wrong?"

"Nothing. Everything's right." He raised his bushy eyebrows as if he didn't believe me. "Please finish my song."

"*...univirren laulan,
Pane pikku simmu kiinni
ja nuku Herran rauhaan.*"

186

Papa whispered good night and slipped out of my room.

Something twigged in my memory—a phrase from the letter, the second page. I hadn't been able to look at the part about Lucy-Jane again, but I'd read the last half of the letter over and over.

I reached into the top dresser drawer and pulled out the crinkly papers. There it was, in the last line of the passage Mr. Blackwell had written: "...*he will joy over thee with singing.*"

The first Finnish immigrants to Canada arrived in the 1870s and settled in the Thunder Bay area. By 1913, about one out of every ten people living in Port Arthur (now part of Thunder Bay), Ontario, was of Finnish origin. They chose the area for its employment opportunities and for the similarity of its landscape to their homeland. Finnish immigrants kept their language and culture alive. They were involved in their community, choosing from a variety of activities including Finnish church congregations, the temperance movement, drama, music, sports, and labour organization. There is still a strong Finnish component to Thunder Bay. The Finnish Labour Temple, now called the Finlandia Club, hosts the Thunder Bay Finnish Canadian Historical Society museum, the Hoito Restaurant, and community social events in "the big Finn Hall."

The Canadian Pacific steamship *Empress of Ireland* began service as an Atlantic liner in 1906. Over the following eight years, the *Empress* transported more than 117,000 passengers to Canada, many of whom were emigrants en route to settle in Canada's western provinces. On the ninety-sixth voyage, sailing from the city of Quebec to Liverpool, England, the *Empress of Ireland* was struck by the Norwegian coal ship *Storstad*. The collision occurred in thick St. Lawrence River fog during the early morning of Friday, May 29, 1914. The *Empress* was equipped with adequate safety features (a response to the *Titanic*'s demise in 1912); however, because of insufficient time and excessive listing, the crew was unable to launch all of the lifeboats or close all of the watertight doors. After only fourteen minutes, the *Empress of Ireland* sank. Of the 1,477 people on board, 1,012 died. The event remains Canada's worst maritime disaster in peacetime.

CATEGORY	ON BOARD	RESCUED
First Class	87	36 (41%)
First-class Children	4	1
Second Class	253	48 (19%)
Second-class Children	32	2
Third Class	717	133 (19%)
Third-class Children	102	1
Passengers Destined for Finland	91	21 (23%)
Crew	420	248 (59%)

Among the passengers were celebrities such as actor Laurence Irving, his wife, actress Mabel Hackney, and

British explorer Sir Henry Seton-Karr (none of whom survived). Members of the Salvation Army were travelling to London for an International Congress. The exact number is uncertain, but of approximately 170 Salvationists, 29 were rescued. Most of the passengers on the *Empress of Ireland* were in third class, and most of them were first-generation immigrants, called "foreigners," returning to their homelands. Tragically, of the 138 children on board, only 4 survived.

The outbreak of the First World War, two months after the sinking, overshadowed the tragedy. The *Empress of Ireland* was largely forgotten—except by crew and passengers who had sailed on the steamship, survivors of the sinking and their descendants, the victims' families, the Salvation Army, and the people of Quebec. The last known survivor of the *Empress* disaster, Grace Martyn (née Hanagan), died in May of 1995.

Rediscovering the location of the wreck in 1964 revived interest in the vessel. The *Empress* lies northeast of Rimouski, 45 metres below the surface, and was declared a national historical site by the Government of Canada in 1999. The wreck is accessible only to expert divers because of the cold water, strong river current, and poor visibility. The remains of hundreds of people are still contained within the ship.

Most of the artifacts recovered from the wreck are in the hands of private collectors. The *Empress of Ireland* Artifacts Committee is dedicated to acquiring important artifacts and donating them for public exhibition in Canada. At the Musée de la mer in Pointe-au-Père,

Quebec, there is a collection of salvaged *Empress of Ireland* artifacts and a 3-D multimedia re-enactment of the disaster.

Further information about the *Empress of Ireland* and the ship's artifacts can be found in the resources listed below.

Canadian Pacific: The Story of the Famous Shipping Line, by George Musk

Empress of Ireland: The Story of an Edwardian Liner, by Derek Grout

Forgotten Empress, by David Zeni

Ghostliners: Exploring The World's Greatest Lost Ships, by Robert D. Ballard and Rick Archbold

www.museedelamer.qc.ca

www.lostliners.com/Liners/Canadian_Pacific/Empress_Ireland

www.sea-viewdiving.com/shipwreck_info/empress_of_ireland1.htm

www.empressartifacts.org

Kivelä Bakery, 111 Secord Street, Port Arthur, with employees
and horse-drawn delivery wagons out front (early 1900s).
— LAKEHEAD UNIVERSITY ARCHIVES, THUNDER BAY FINNISH CANADIAN
HISTORICAL SOCIETY COLLECTION MG 8, D, 1, 1, C, I, 1

The cast of a play produced by the Finnish Drama Society in Port
Arthur (early 1900s). — LAKEHEAD UNIVERSITY ARCHIVES, FINLANDIA CLUB
COLLECTION MG 3, XIII, 54

Notice who is holding the reins! The photograph was taken in the early 1900s somewhere in the countryside near Port Arthur, perhaps in North Branch where Saara's aunt and uncle had their homestead. — LAKEHEAD UNIVERSITY ARCHIVES, FINLANDIA CLUB COLLECTION MG 3, XIII, 49

Mr. A. Kivistö and Mrs. Hilma (Pantila) Kivistö of Port Arthur, circa 1900. Mrs. Kivistö and her two children perished in the *Empress of Ireland* disaster on May 29, 1914. — LAKEHEAD UNIVERSITY ARCHIVES, THUNDER BAY FINNISH CANADIAN HISTORICAL SOCIETY COLLECTION MG 8, D, 1, 1, F, I, 13

Men, women, and children gathered in front of the Finnish
Labour Temple in Port Arthur to celebrate its opening in 1910.
— IMAGE REPRODUCED FROM COVERS OF *Project Bay Street: Activities of Finnish-
Canadians in Thunder Bay Before 1915*, COURTESY THUNDER BAY FINNISH
CANADIAN HISTORICAL SOCIETY

The *Empress of Ireland* at the Breakwater, city of Quebec (between
1906 and 1913). — COURTESY STEPHEN BROOKS

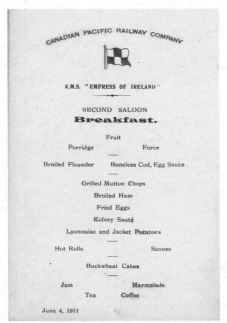

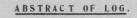

	ABSTRACT OF LOG.	

R.M.S. "EMPRESS of IRELAND."

J. V. FORSTER, R.N.R. COMMANDER.

——o——

St. John, N.B. to Liverpool 30th November, 1907.
VIA HALIFAX

Left   Halifax   1-28 A.M.   December   1st

DATE.	DIST.	LAT.N.	LONG.W.	REMARKS
Dec. 1	184	45.06	59.20	Moderate wind & choppy head sea.
,, 2	407	37.41	59.20	Strong head wind and rough sea.
,, 3	417	51.05	41.06	Strong to fresh wind, following sea
,, 4	400	53.37	31.08	Strong quarterly gale, high following sea.
,, 5	412	55.24	19.43	Strong quarterly wind, heavy sea
,, 6	425	55.28	7.20½	Fresh following wind, heavy confused sea
	195	To Bar Lightship		
Total	2440			

Arrived Bar Lightship   11-26 P.M.   Friday, December 6th, 1907
Passage, Halifax to Liverpool   5 days,   17 hour,   58 minutes
Average   Speed   17.68   knots

An Abstract of Log postcard from the *Empress of Ireland*, 1907.
— COURTESY STEPHEN BROOKS

Empress of Ireland second-class saloon breakfast menu, June 4, 1911.
— COURTESY STEPHEN BROOKS

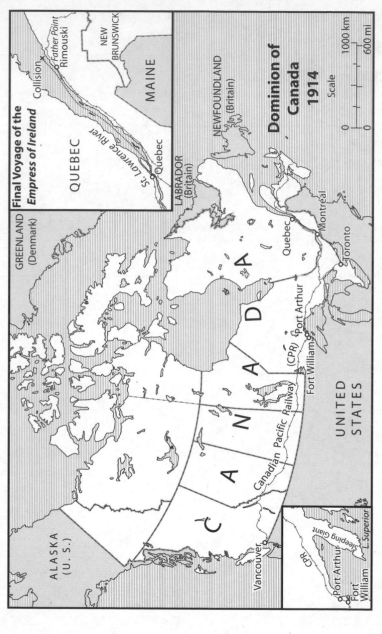

The Canadian Pacific Railway and final voyage of the Canadian Pacific steamship *Empress of Ireland*, 1914. Saara's route took her from Port Arthur to the city of Quebec, then up the St. Lawrence River on the *Empress of Ireland*.

ACKNOWLEDGEMENTS

Numerous people assisted me in the creation of this book and I wish to thank all of them. In particular, thank you to the staff at the Thunder Bay Museum, the Brodie Resource Library, and the Mission Branch of the Okanagan Regional Library; Stephen Lyons of Canadian Pacific Archives; Louise Wuorinen and Trudy Mauracher at the Chancellor Paterson Library at Lakehead University; Don and Regina Hannula for resource material about Thunder Bay; Margett Goward, Ilkka Koskivuo, and Vesa Koskivuo for help with Finnish language questions; Marion Kelch, chairperson of the *Empress of Ireland* Artifacts Committee, for sharing her vast knowledge about and passion for the *Empress*; Lyyli Repo for all I learned from her about Finnish immigrant life in Port Arthur and on her family's homestead; Tyyne Marja-aho and Esteri Ylinen for their childhood memories, especially for the song Tyyne's father sang to her that became "Saara's song."

I would like to thank Karl R. Larson, secretary of the Salvation Army Archives, for research assistance and reviewing the manuscript for historical accuracy concerning the Salvation Army; Derek Grout, author of *Empress of Ireland: The Story of an Edwardian Liner*, for reviewing the manuscript for accuracy regarding the *Empress of Ireland*; Beverly Soloway, for reviewing the manuscript for historical accuracy regarding Finnish-Canadian culture in Port Arthur and area; and Kathryn Bridge and Robert D. Turner, for reviewing the manuscript for historical accuracy.

Many thanks to Helen Berarducci, Cynthia Boldt, Lucille Charlton, Irene Failes, Varpu Lindström, Rhea and Mala Milanese, Rosemary Nelson, and Lillian Wolter for helpful feedback; and the members of the CompuServe Literary Forum's Private Kidcrit section for their support and invaluable critiques, especially Malcolm Campbell, Kate Coombs, Anita Daher, Cali Doxiadis, Karen Dyer, Liz Gaspar, Linda Gerber, Julie Kentner, Janet McConnaughey, Polly Martin, Helen Mulligan, Rosemarie Riechel, Bonnie Sauder, Marsha Skrypuch, and Lynne Supeene.

I am grateful to Nikki Tate and Andrea Spalding for their ongoing support as mentors, and to my fellow writers Fiona Bayrock, Patricia Fazackerley, Patricia Fraser, Eileen Holland, Mary Ann Thompson, and Leah Todd, for their encouraging words and practical advice.

Sincere thanks to my friends and colleagues Sharon Helberg and Loraine Kemp for their continuous support, multiple critiques of the manuscript, and longstanding confidence that this book would be published; my sister, Kathy Pelletier, for her research assistance; and my grandmother, Hilja Lange, for sharing her early memories of Finnish-Canadian life in the Thunder Bay area. *Kiitos paljon* to my grandparents Aili and Eino Ala—Mummu and Pappa—for teaching me about my Finnish heritage, for the gift of the spoon that led me to write this story, and for sharing memories of their early years. To my parents, Art and Anita Lange, my heartfelt thanks for your encouragement to follow my dream, help with researching Finnish-Canadian life in 1914, and patience with my questions about Finnish customs and language. To my husband, Will, and my children, Annaliis and Stefan, an enormous thank you for the many ways that you supported me in my writing and for your unwavering belief in me and this book.

I would also like to thank my editor, Laura Peetoom, for her keen insight and warm guidance throughout the editing process; my copy editor, Dawn Loewen, for her first-class work attending to details; and my publisher, Diane Morriss, for her constant support and enthusiasm.

Karen Autio in period costume, holding artifacts from the *Empress of Ireland*: a third-class mineral water bottle and deep plate (complete with white barnacle), both salvaged from the wreck, as well as a lime that washed ashore in a crate from the ship.

Karen Autio likes to keep company with words, whether as a writer, reader, or calligrapher. She also likes to collect objects with stories, such as a wind-up watch that's older than she is and an antique desk that *might* have secret compartments. When Karen's Finnish grandmother gave her a silver spoon and told her its tale, Karen had no idea it would lead her into a whole novel's worth of words. She learned that her grandmother's Finnish friends had family members from Port Arthur (now part of Thunder Bay) who died in the wreck of the *Empress of Ireland*. Karen researched the steamship and wove the ship's story into fictional Saara's life.

Karen grew up in the Thunder Bay area and now lives in Kelowna, B.C., with her husband and two children. *Second Watch* is her first book.

To learn more about the story behind Saara and the *Empress of Ireland*, visit www.karenautio.com.